COWBOY D-FORCE

BROTHERHOOD PROTECTORS BOOK #4

ELLE JAMES

TWISTED PAGE INC.

COWBOY D-FORCE

BROTHERHOOD PROTECTORS
BOOK #4

New York Times & *USA Today*
Bestselling Author

ELLE JAMES

EBOOK ISBN: 978-1-62695-155-6

PRINT ISBN: 978-1-62695-156-3

This story is dedicated to my readers who keep me writing by buying my books. I love what I do, and I hope you love it, too. Thank you so much for your continued support!
I'd also like to thank my sister and editor, Delilah Devlin, who keeps me in commas.

Elle James

AUTHOR'S NOTE

Enjoy other military books by Elle James

Visit ellejames.com for more titles and release dates
For hot cowboys, visit her alter ego Myla Jackson
at mylajackson.com
and join Elle James's Newsletter at
https://ellejames.com/contact/

CHAPTER 1

JOHN WAYNE MORRISON turned on his barstool and surveyed the occupants of the Blue Moose Tavern in Eagle Rock, Montana, trying to remember how to behave like a civilian.

In one corner of the room, a group of rangy cowboys gathered around the back corner, flipping quarters at a rattlesnake that had the misfortune of finding its way into the bar.

"Here's your beer." The burly bartender banged a mug full of lager on the bar, sloshing some over the top. He glanced at the dusty cowboys and yelled, "Hey, get that snake out of my bar!" Then he muttered under his breath, "Damned fools. Someone's gonna get hurt. You'd think they'd have more sense."

"Are rattlesnakes part of the entertainment around here?" John asked.

The bartender wiped the spilled beer off the counter. "Slow night." His eyes narrowed. "You're new around here. I'm Butch." The man held out a meaty hand. "Got a name?"

"Name's John Morrison, but my friends call me Duke." He gripped the man's hand and shook. Used to strong grips from his former Delta-Force team, he wasn't prepared for the bartender to choke the crap out of his hand. Increasing the strength on his own grasp, he didn't let go until the bartender loosened his grip first and released.

"Duke, huh?" Butch flexed his fingers and went back to filling mugs with beer. "Your middle name happen to be Wayne?"

Resigned to the usual ribbing he got when he gave anyone his full name, Duke nodded. "As a matter of fact, it is. My father was a big fan of old western movies. Stuck me with John Wayne."

"Makes sense to go by Duke."

"Yeah. It's hard to avoid." Duke took a long pull on his drink, letting the cool liquid glide down his throat. The drive from Ft. Hood, Texas had taken two days across some of the most desolate landscape in the country. Now that he was in Montana, he was looking forward to being near the mountains, hunting, fishing and riding horses. Hell, he hadn't been on a horse since he'd joined the army over twelve years ago.

"So, what brings you to Eagle Rock?" Butch asked.

Duke snorted. "Coming home to Montana."

"Coming home? Where ya been?'

"Military." His gut tightened, and his knee throbbed. For the past twelve years, he'd dedicated his life to protecting and serving the nation.

"Branch?" the bartender queried.

"Army."

"Prior marine, myself," Butch said. "Deploy?"

Duke nodded.

"See much action?"

Again, Duke nodded, not offering any more information. Most of his deployments had been Top Secret. Only those with a need to know, and with the requisite clearance, knew about those missions. The last one had been so secret that only the Secretary of State and the President had known of its existence.

"You don't talk much, do you?" Butch raised his hand. "Not that I mind. Most cowboys drink a few beers and expect me to be some kind of free therapist. From difficulties with their bosses, to woman troubles, I've heard it all." The bartender resumed wiping the bar. "You're a freakin' breath of fresh air. You just sit right there and fill a quiet space at my bar."

Duke gave him a hint of a smile and went back to drinking his beer and people-watching.

One of the younger patrons stuck some money in the jukebox, and a cry-in-your-beer song came on. Several cowboys led their ladies onto the small dance floor near an empty stage.

The beer, the music and the laid-back atmosphere soothed Duke's tired soul. After he finished his beer, he'd walk back to the bed and breakfast where he was staying the night. Tomorrow, he'd check in with his new boss, Hank Patterson, at the White Oak Ranch. From there, he'd report to his first assignment as personal security to someone wealthy enough to pay for protection.

As the song ended, so too did his beer. He pushed to his feet and was digging in his pocket for his wallet, when his cell phone buzzed.

He glanced down and grinned when he saw an incoming FaceTime call from Rider, one of his buddies from his former unit at Ft. Hood. He accepted the call. "Hey, dirtbag. Miss me already?"

Blaze, leaned into view beside Rider. "Damn right, we miss you. When are you going to come to your senses and get back to work?"

Rider shoved Blaze away and grinned into the phone. "Just making sure you got there all right. The team isn't the same without you."

His chest tightened. He'd hated leaving the men who'd come to feel like brothers. "Yeah, well, you'll do fine without me. You need fresh meat to pound into shape."

"No, we like the old meat we can count on to have our backs," Blaze said, his face appearing over Rider's shoulder.

"When do you start your new job?" Rider asked.

"Tomorrow," Duke said. "I meet with the head of Brotherhood Protectors, Hank Patterson. Want me to put in a good word for you?"

"Hell, yeah," Rider said. "Never know when this gig will play out. And I'm not getting any younger."

"You'd better check with Briana before you commit to a move to Montana. It gets cold up here in the winter."

Rider nodded. "Will do. You know the gang is due some time off. We might try to make it up there in the near future. I hear the fly fishing is pretty good up your way."

Duke laughed. "What do you know about fly fishing?"

"Nothing, but that's why we keep you around. To show us how to do things"

"Yeah. Well you know I'd always be glad to see any one of you."

"Done," Rider said. "As soon as we can get some leave approved."

"Good. I think you'd like it here. And you're right, the fly fishing is the best."

"I knew it." Rider grinned. "In the meantime, let us know if you get in a bind and need us to bail you out of a bad situation."

"Or a county jail," Blaze added. "And if you find any hot babes in the backwoods, give them my number." He smirked. "As long as they have all of their teeth."

"Will do," Duke said. "I'll be sure to show them that picture I took of you at our last unit picnic."

Rider laughed. "I'm sure the ladies will all want a piece of the cross-dressing, hairy-legged grandma."

Blaze frowned. "I don't suppose you'll ever let me live that one down, will you?"

Duke shook his head. "Not a chance."

"Well, I can mark Montana women off my list as long, as the Duke is flashing his blackmail photo."

"No, seriously, Duke," Rider said, "if you need us, all you have to do is pick up a phone."

"Thanks. It's nice to know I still have friends, even if they're two days away."

"Later," Rider said.

"Later." He rang off with a smile still tugging at his lips and glanced up in time to notice a commotion at the entrance.

A man wearing a windbreaker backed into the room with his camera balanced on his shoulder and aimed at the open doorway.

Curious, Duke handed his credit card over to the bartender and turned back in time to see a blonde strut through the door.

She wore sunglasses, despite it being dark

outside and not much lighter inside. She'd gone maybe five steps when she tripped over her own feet, teetered on impossibly high heels and pitched into the camera man.

He fell back on his ass, holding his camera in the air to keep it from bouncing on the hardwood floor.

The blonde, who'd managed to regain her balance, straightened her jacket, tilted her sunglasses and glanced down at the camera man. "Move, you clumsy idiot!"

Two cowboys grabbed the man's shoulders, hauled him to his feet and let go.

"Sorry, Miss Love," he said. "Didn't mean to get in your way." Without missing another beat, he raised his camera to his shoulder and continued filming.

The woman's mouth twisted into a sneer. She planted her hand in the lens of his camera and pushed past the man, nearly knocking him off his feet again.

She made for the bar, dropped her huge, designer bag on the counter and ordered, "Mango martini. Vodka. Shaken, not stirred." She raised two fingers. "Make that two."

Then she tilted her head downward, looked over the top of her sunglasses at Duke and raised her brows. "Mmm. If the men all look like you, I might learn to like Montana."

Duke saw no need to comment. She wasn't his type—too trashed and too high-maintenance. If he had his credit card back, he would leave the diva and go find a bed to crash in.

"This is the only place I've found to get a decent drink in this godforsaken shithole of a town." She perched one cheek on the barstool and leaned her back against the counter. "I'll be glad to get back to LA in a week." She laid her hand on his arm, digging her nails into his shirt. "Please tell me you're not from around here. I need to talk to someone who hasn't hit his head on the ground so many times he's nothing more than a toothless idiot."

"Sorry. I'm from Montana." Duke's lips twitched. "However, I do have my teeth." He grinned to prove it.

The bartender served the two martinis. Then he leaned close and whispered, "You do realize that's Lena Love, don't you? You're damned lucky, you are."

Duke wasn't feeling all that lucky. The woman next to him hadn't given up her claw-like hold on his arm yet.

Balancing herself against him, she downed first one martini then the other.

"Damned watered-down drinks. Can't even cop a buzz." She raised her hand. "Two more please, only this time, don't skimp on the vodka." She dug into her voluminous purse, extracted a bottle of pills, shook out two and threw the bottle back inside. "This place smells like sweaty men." She leaned close to Duke and sniffed. "You smell like a sweaty man." She licked his neck. "Mmm, you taste salty."

Duke jerked back, his skin crawling at the woman's behavior. He had the sudden urge to take a shower.

The bartender set her martinis on the counter.

She tossed the pills into her mouth and chased them with the first martini. "That's more like it." Without missing a beat, she chugged her fourth martini and turned toward the dance floor.

"Doesn't anyone know how to party around here?" She shook her head and dug into her purse again. When she couldn't find what she was looking for, she shouted, "Phillip. I need two dollars."

A man dressed in a business suit materialized out of the crowd. "Lena, don't you think we should leave now that you've had your drinks?"

"Fuck no." She held out her hand and wiggled her fingers. "Two dollars, dammit."

Phillip pulled two dollar bills from his own wallet and handed them over.

Lena slapped them on the counter. "Quarters."

Butch glared at the woman, but changed the dollars for quarters, tossing them on the counter.

"Insolent bastard," Lena muttered. She grabbed the change and slid off the stool, nearly falling off her high heels in the process. With one hand on Duke's knee, she pulled herself upright, winked at him and swayed across the floor to the jukebox.

Dropping all eight quarters into the juke box, she bent over the glass top, her bottom, wrapped in a skin-tight skirt that barely covered the necessities, rocking back and forth to the country tune playing. After selecting several songs, she straightened and waited for the first one to begin.

Her head bobbed to the tune, and she looked around the room full of cowboys, who were standing back to see what this woman would do next.

Apparently, she didn't see in any of them whatever it was she was looking for, until she spotted Duke again. Her eyes narrowed, and she stalked toward him, weaving through the array of tables and long-legged men.

"Butch, I'll be needing my credit card," Duke muttered, his pulse picking up, his anxiety level ratcheting to higher than when he'd stepped out in an ISIS-held town. He did not want to be at the bar or anywhere else in the room when the diva made it across the floor. The only thing slowing her down were her high heels and all the alcohol and pills she'd consumed. "Credit card, Butch. Now."

Butch slapped the card and slip of paper on the

counter. "She's coming for you, man. That's Lena Love, the actress."

"I wouldn't care if she was bringing me winning lottery numbers. She's trouble." Duke turned away long enough to scribble his name on the bottom line and grab his card. When he glanced up again, he realized he was too late.

Miss Love stood directly in front him, her breasts thrust out, her eyelids seductively lowered and her hand outstretched. "You. Dance floor. Now."

He held up his hands. "Sorry, ma'am. I don't dance." Especially not with women higher than the Empire State Building.

She blinked, the seductive look disappearing and in its place something akin to shock.

Had no one ever said *no* to the woman?

"Excuse me. I was just leaving." He tried to step around her, but she shifted to the side, blocking his path.

"No one says no to Lena Love."

"Life is full of firsts. Get used to them." He tried dodging in the other direction.

For a drunk high on pills and alcohol, she moved fast, again blocking his path.

The cameraman stood to one side, filming the entire exchange.

Duke shot him an annoyed glare and then returned his gaze to the woman. "Look, Miss Love,

I've been on the road for two days. I'm tired and not in the mood to play games."

"Just one dance," she begged. "That's all I'm asking."

"Not interested."

"Perhaps you'd be interested in this."

Before he could even guess what she'd do next, Duke received the full impact of two perfectly matching Double-D sized breasts, naked as the day they'd been implanted, full-on, in front of God and everyone in that bar.

He stood in stunned silence, unable to comprehend what had just happened.

Cowboys throughout the room hooted and threw their hats into the air. Then the chanting started. "More! More! More!"

"That's right, baby! Take it all off," one redneck shouted.

Wolf calls and whistles charged the air, piercing Duke's eardrums.

He took hold of Lena's hands and pulled them down, taking the hem of her shirt with them, covering her boobs. "Seriously, I'm not interested now—or ever. Please, just get out of my way." He gripped her arms and physically lifted her to set her to the side. Then he left her standing there, her jaw hanging, her eyes narrowing into tiny slits.

If he didn't get out of there quickly, the woman might launch herself at him, and he might be forced to break one of the rules his mother had drilled into his head as a young cowboy. Never hit a woman. His vision narrowed and buzzing filled his head. Sweat glazed his palms. He hadn't felt this trapped since he'd been pinned down in a collapsed building in a godforsaken Afghan village.

He made it through the room and out the door. As soon as he was outside, he broke into a sprint toward his truck, climbed in and hauled ass out of the parking lot and away from the obnoxious diva he wanted no part of.

So much for a relaxing reintroduction to his beloved state of Montana. Hopefully, his second day back home would be better than his first.

CHAPTER 2

THE BANGING on her Jeep window jolted Angel out of the nice nap she'd just started. Normally, her boss, Lena, managed to stay longer than thirty minutes in a bar. Angel had been counting on at least that long of a nap.

Except Lena's publicist was pounding the glass, his face a study of desperation. What was Lena up to now?

Angel sighed and lowered the window. "What's up, Phil?"

"She's doing it again. And there's a cameraman inside getting it all on video."

"Get her out," Angel said, rolling the window up.

Phillip clutched the top of the glass as it whirred upward, trying to keep it from closing. "You gotta help me. We need damage control before that video gets out. And she just flashed a stranger. It's all on the god damn video!"

"That's your problem. I'm just the stunt double. I'm not even sure why you brought me along." She shrugged. "Don't really care as long as I get paid an indecent amount of money."

His eyes widened. "Seriously, if you want a paycheck, you have to help me get her out before she kills her chance at any future scripts because she's such a loose cannon."

Angel sighed. Phillip seemed a nice enough guy, but he worked for the bitchiest, most narcissistic woman in Hollywood. Which said a lot, considering Lena lived in Hollywood among hundreds of actress wannabes, who thought they were God's gift to the silver screen. Lord help those who didn't agree.

But Lena was the drama queen to beat all drama queens.

"What's she done now?" How she'd gone from being a respectable stunt woman to Lena Love's body double, on the screen and off, she wasn't sure. Then again, she did know. The money was pretty damned good. Another year and she could afford to buy her own house in the woods and pay cash. Then she could work in a library or an oil change place. Somewhere she didn't have to hurl her body through glass windows or ride motorcycles through flames

"She just flashed one of the customers because he refused to dance with her."

"I like the man already." Angel pulled the keys from the ignition, climbed out of the car and followed Phillip to the door.

She didn't like loud music, and she liked cowboys even less. They usually smelled like horses. And she really didn't like horses. Not since she'd tried stunt riding for Lena. The horse had spooked when one of the booms had fallen to the ground with a loud crash.

Angel had thought she was going to die that day. Three miles later, after jumping a fence, crossing a six-lane highway and crashing into someone's back yard pool, the horse had finally slowed enough for Angel to jump off. How the horse wrangler had gotten the animal out of the swimming pool, she still didn't know. She'd almost drowned along with the animal and had to suffer through a trip to the hospital in the back of an ambulance with a suicidal driver.

She drew her stunt assignments line at horse-back riding. And she was about to tell Lena where she could put her big, fat paychecks.

With her blond hair tucked up in a baseball cap, and wearing a baggy hoody and equally baggy jeans, Angel could have passed for a teen from the hood, instead of a woman, with the right makeup and hairstyle, was the spitting image of

Lena Love, multi-million-dollar princess of the big screen.

Lucky her. When she wasn't careful, she was stopped in stores around LA, mistaken for the actress. Having the paparazzi follow her gave her a real understanding of what it was like to be famous.

Lena could have it. It wasn't Angel's circus, and she didn't want anything to do with the publicity.

Unfortunately, she'd been called in on several occasions to "be" Lena when Lena was indisposed and couldn't represent herself—code for stoned out of her mind or passed out cold.

"Damn it, where'd she go?" Phillip stood on his toes, searching the room for the blonde. "She was at the bar when I went outside."

"I'll check the ladies room," Angel said. "You check outside the back door."

Phillip ran for the back of the building and hopefully a rear exit.

Angel hoped Phillip would find Lena first, and save her from telling the woman what she thought of her troubled life. She wasn't afraid to speak her mind to Lena. Wouldn't matter anyway. When she sobered up, Lena would have no memory of what Angel had said.

She followed the sign indicating the direction for the restrooms and entered a darkened hallway.

She'd seen far too many scary movies to like dark hallways. Nothing good ever happened in them.

With a firm mental shove, she pushed her misgivings to the side, pressed on and entered the ladies' room to find the space in complete darkness. Angel ran her hand along the wall, located the light switch and flipped it on.

At first, she thought the bathroom was empty. She turned to leave, but stopped when she heard a slight moan.

"Lena?" she called out.

Another moan sounded. Angel ducked low, looking under the stall doors for legs and feet. In the last one, she found more than legs and feet. She found Lena, lying on the floor in front of the toilet, her back to Angel.

Angel tried the stall door, but it was locked. "Lena, you have to get up and unlock the door."

Another moan, but no movement on the actress's part.

"Jesus, Lena, if you're going to pass out, at least leave the freakin' door unlocked." Angel shot a glance to the ceiling, knowing what she had to do and not liking it one bit. She didn't mind rolling in the dirt, wearing a fire-retardant suit and being doused in gasoline and set on fire, but she really hated touching anything in a public restroom, especially the floors around the toilets.

Yanking several paper towels out of the

dispenser, she placed them on the ground in front of the stall door. With a deep breath, she lay on her back and shimmied beneath the stall door, bumping up against Lena's inert body.

The woman moved, groaned and heaved her guts up all over the nasty floor. Now, not only did it smell like urine, the restroom smelled like booze vomit.

Fighting the urge to retch, Angel worked her way into the stall, stood, unlocked the door and flung it open. Then she reached to hook her hands beneath Lena's arms and dragged her away from the toilet and into the middle of the washroom.

That's when she saw it.

"Sweet Jesus, that can't be good." Struggling with the smell and the urge to contribute to it, Angel stepped to the door and opened it. "Phillip, you gotta see this."

Phillip glanced up at the sign over the door. "I can't go into the ladies' restroom."

"Make an exception. We have a problem."

He shot a look down the hallway, and then ducked through the door. "Make it quick. What's wrong—holy shit! What the hell happened?"

"Apparently, someone didn't like Lena flashing her boobs, or she's got a stalker."

BITCH was written across Lena's forehead in big, black, bold letters. Also, trailing down one cheek were the words, *I'm going to make*, and on the other, *you pay*.

A shiver rippled across Angel's skin, raising goose bumps. She ran to the sink, wet a fresh paper towel and bent to wipe the ink from Lena's face.

The wet paper towel did nothing to remove the ink. She tried adding soap to the towel. The soap had no more effect than the water.

"Sweet Jesus," Phillip said. "What are we going to do now? She can't be seen in public like that."

"Seriously? That's all you're worried about?" Angel pointed at the writing. "That's a threat. And apparently, whoever did it has it in for Miss Love. This ink is not coming off."

Phillip stood, wringing his hands. "She can't leave this bathroom like that."

"As it is, she's not going out on her own two feet anyway. She can't stand up and walk back through the barroom. The woman needs to be carried out."

Phillip tried to lift Lena into his arms, but like a slippery fish, the actress slid through his fingers. "The camera man is waiting to catch anything he can on Lena. She's already had too much negative publicity."

"I thought any publicity, good or bad, was preferable to no publicity."

"Yeah, ask Lindsay Lohan how that worked for her. Or Brittany Spears. Sometimes it works in their favor, but not always. Talent only gets you so far. Being easy to work with gets you the roles. She's got too much riding on a script she really wants. It's a juicy one that could position her for an Oscar nomination. The studio doesn't want a mess on their hands."

"And she's a mess." Angel murmured. "I've seen her party too hard, but this takes it further. Does she need to go into a rehab center?"

Phillip sighed. "I've tried to talk her into it, but she doesn't think she has a problem."

"Passed out drunk in a bathroom stall is a problem. Whoever did that to her face could have done a whole lot worse."

"She needs a keeper," Phillip said.

Angel held up her hands. "Don't look at me. I'm just a stunt woman, not a bodyguard."

Phillip's eyes narrowed. "You know, you're more valuable as her double than as her bodyguard. This might be the perfect timing to get her into a private rehab facility. She could be detoxing while you're flushing out the jerk who did this to her." His lips spread into a genuine grin and he rubbed his hands together.

"Me? Play the part of Lena Love in real life?" Angel flung her hands in the air and backed away. "Oh, no. I'm all good for taking the hits, driving the fast cars, falling through the windows, but I'm no actress."

"I've seen you mimic Lena's tantrums. That's all

you have to do. Please, stay on her ranch for the next two weeks while we clean up her face and dry her out."

Angel frowned. "What about the message on Lena's face? Someone's got it out for her."

"So, you're bait for the nutcase who did this. We'll hire a bodyguard for you, since the world will think you're Lena."

"I'm not so sure I like being bait. And I don't need a bodyguard."

"At least, you'll stay sober. You won't be caught off guard like Lena. And I know you can defend yourself with your military background. But a bodyguard is something Lean would want."

"She has bodyguards. Though, where were they when she was attacked here in the restroom?"

"Something I plan to find out. I'm not impressed with their abilities. Plus, we need one who isn't as familiar with Lena as her own body-guards. I'll check around the state for someone local."

Angel thought about what Phillip was telling her. "So, all I have to do is play Lena, on her ranch, here in Montana, not LA?"

"Two weeks."

"I'll have full use of the pool and everything, just like Lena?" Angel was warming to the idea.

He nodded. "Everything, even her wardrobe."

"And Lena will be off somewhere in a rehab facility? I don't have to put up with her bullshit?"

Phillip held up two fingers. "Scouts honor."

Angel snorted. "Like you were ever a scout." She made up her mind. "Okay. I'll be Lena for two weeks. Other than an artistic stalker who paints threats on actress's faces, it sounds like the perfect paid vacation." She held out her hand. "Deal."

"Deal." Phillip shook her hand. "I'll have a body-guard sent out to Love Land tomorrow."

Angel shrugged. "No hurry. I wouldn't want him to get in the way of my downtime."

At that moment, Lena moaned, opened her eyes and said, "Where am I?" Then her eyes rolled to the back of her head, and she passed out again.

"Let's get sleeping beauty out of here," Angel said.

"Yeah, and whatever you do, don't let anyone see us carrying out a passed out drunk Lena Love."

Angel pulled a bright pink camouflage bandana from the hip pocket of her jeans and wrapped it around Lena's signature blond hair.

Phillip tried again to lift Miss Love. "I can't do this on my own. I'm not built to haul actresses around in my arms."

"You carry the top. I'll lift from the lower end." Angel grabbed Lena's narrow ankles. "Ready?"

With a nod, Phillip grabbed the woman beneath her armpits.

"Lift," Angel said. Though Phillip took the brunt of Lena's weight, Angel strained against the dead weight. "Where to?"

Phillip tipped his head toward the rear of the building. "There's an emergency exit at the end of the hallway. We can take her out the back."

"I'm ready when you are," he said, his voice tight.

"Good, let's get her out of here."

Phillip backed all the way down the hall, through the exit, and out into the starlit, Montana sky.

So far, so good. They might get her out of the bar for the night, but how would they get the indelible ink off her face?

Angel figured that would be Phillip's problem to tackle when Lena was in detox.

For the next two weeks, Angel had a date with a swimming pool and fruity cocktails she could slip some whiskey into. Playing the rich and arrogant Lena Love could be fun, as long as her new bodyguard and the artistic stalker didn't rain on her summer sunshine.

CHAPTER 3

D<small>UKE</small> <small>PULLED</small> up to the gate of the Love Land Ranch and shook his head. He couldn't believe his first assignment was as bodyguard to the infamous Lena Love. The eccentric diva who'd flashed her tits at him the night before at the Blue Moose Tavern. Sure, he'd expected to provide personal security to some rich and famous person, but holy shit.

Not her.

"Is there someone else who can take this one?" he'd asked his new boss, Hank Patterson. Yeah, it might not be the right thing to ask on your first day, but geez, the woman was toxic.

Hank frowned. "I would think you'd be excited to get this gig. Lena Love is iconic in the movie industry."

"She's not the nicest person." Hank's wife, Sadie, entered the room carrying a tiny bundle, their little girl, born only two months previously.

Although he'd just met the man, obviously, in Hank's book, the baby hung the moon. And the man was extraordinarily loving toward his wife.

Sadie pursed her lips. "I was on the same set with Lena once. I swore I'd never do another movie with her. She's one-hundred-percent diva and a real beyotch." Sadie McClain would know. Having established herself as one of Hollywood's top-grossing actresses, she was Lena's direct competition.

Hank arched an eyebrow. "The assignment is short term. Two weeks. When she goes back to LA, she'll return to using her own bodyguards." Hank fixed his gaze on Duke. "Two weeks. That's all I'm asking. I'd take it myself, but I've got a couple more guys coming on board soon, and I've been out beating the bushes for clients."

"Not to mention, you're on diaper duty this weekend. when I have to be at the premier of my new movie." Sadie stared down at her baby. "Isn't that right, Emma, sweetheart? Daddy has diaper duty."

Hank's lips twisted. "You heard her. I'm tied up this weekend, and all my other agents are assigned. You're the only man I have who can take this one. I have another job coming up, but the client has yet to arrive in country. The timing of this assignment keeps you employed until he arrives." Hank tilted his head. "What have you got against Ms. Love?"

"She made a pass at me last night and gave me a full-frontal exposure of her manufactured breasts."

"She flashed you?" Hank's bark of laughter startled the baby.

Emma cried out.

"Shh, sweet Emma," Sadie sang to soothe the baby back to sleep. "Hank, really," she admonished her husband.

"Two weeks. That's all I ask," Hank said in his inside voice, a smile tugging at his lips.

His first assignment with the Brotherhood Protectors and he already wanted out of it.

Duke stared up at the arched sign and sighed. From bad-ass Delta Force soldier to babysitting a spoiled, obnoxious diva. He'd sunk to a new level of low he'd never expected.

Maybe he would be better off hiring out as a cowboy for room and board on a corporate cattle ranch. At least, he wouldn't have women flashing him.

His mother would be appalled at Miss Love's behavior. He'd just have to keep that little tidbit about the flashing to himself.

Duke blamed his mother for his lack of permanent relationships with the opposite sex. His mother had been the consummate housewife, mother and nurturer. She was the best cook, most accomplished seamstress and the nicest person he had the pleasure of knowing. How could any woman measure up to her perfection?

Yeah, he'd had sex with a number of willing participants, but he'd always found something about them that didn't quite make the cut.

Now. This woman.

Two weeks.

He'd survived for two weeks in the hills of Afghanistan, after being separated from his teammates, living off roots and the wild rabbits he'd snared. Two weeks on a rich woman's resort property would be nothing.

Then why would he rather shoot himself in the foot than face Lena Love again?

He punched in the security code and waited for the gate to open enough he could drive his pickup through.

A wide concrete drive wove through a lodgepole pine forest and up into the foothills of the Crazy Mountains. The trees thinned, exposing lush green pastures filled with grazing horses and cattle. The road climbed upward and emerged near the top of a hill. A massive structure of rock, cedar and glass consumed his view.

This was a cabin in the mountains?

Holy crap.

If he wasn't being forced to babysit the diva, this would be a plush assignment. Then again, he wasn't on vacation, nor would he be lounging by a pool, drinking Mai Tais and eating bon bons.

A muscular man, wearing pressed jeans and an equally clean and pressed white shirt, strode around the side of the house and waved at Duke. "Hired help parks in the servants' lot behind the barn." He pointed to a drive leading around to the back of the house.

Since he was the hired help, Duke followed the man's instructions and drove around to the back of the house and down a slope to a barn bigger than the high school he'd attended. It was by far the biggest barn he'd ever worked around. It could be a convention center or big-city rodeo arena.

He parked his truck next to several others bearing the Love Land Ranch logo.

Reluctantly, he climbed down from the pickup. With a brief glance at the back seat, he decided to leave his duffel bag until he learned where he'd be sleeping for this gig. He assumed he'd stay in the big house with Miss Love. If his task was to keep her safe, he'd have to be close enough to do that.

"Bodyguard?" The young, muscleman appeared beside Duke.

Duke nodded. "That would be me."

The man stuck out his hand. "Brandt Lucas. Foreman."

Duke gripped the man's hand. "Duke Morrison."

"Miss Love is up at the pool. She asked me to send you to her as soon as you arrived."

"Thank you."

"If you need help with anything to do with the ranch, cattle or horses, see me or my assistant foreman, Lyle Sorenson." He nodded toward an older man in faded jeans, an equally faded blue chambray shirt and a dusty cowboy hat.

The older guy pushed a wheelbarrow full of muck from the barn to a pile at the rear of the massive structure. He dumped the load, glanced up and nodded in Duke's direction.

Duke almost laughed. The difference between the younger, clean, muscle-bound man and the older, wiry, dirty one was too obvious.

Miss Love had probably promoted Lucas to Foreman based on his looks, rather than his abilities.

"How many horses does Miss Love keep on the ranch?" Duke asked, just to test his theory.

Mr. Lucas shrugged. "A dozen or so. If you want exact numbers, you can consult Mr. Sorenson. He keeps the books on the animals."

"And what do you do?" Duke asked.

He puffed out his chest and lifted his chin. "I'm

the foreman. I tell the other ranch hands what to do."

Duke swallowed back the laughter threatening to erupt. A real ranch foreman knew, to the head, the number of livestock a ranch had and kept close tabs on additions and losses. He knew how much feed it took to get them through the winter, knew which ones were sickly and which horses got along with the others. He'd never leave it to the ranch hands to manage the herds or care for their health and wellbeing.

Man candy. That was what Brandt Lucas was.

Duke didn't have much respect for a man who didn't earn his keep. But then, he didn't know what Lucas had to do for Miss Love to earn his pay. It might have nothing whatsoever to do with managing the livestock or the crops.

"You can go on up to the house," Brandt said with an easy smile. "Like I said, Miss Love is lying by the pool."

Duke climbed the slope to the big house, admiring the combination of rustic charm and clean, modern lines. He cut through a stand of trees and shrubs that provided a barrier around the stone-paved patio and pool. A rock waterfall graced one end of the pool, and a line of deck chairs stood between the pool and the house. One of which was occupied by a woman wearing a miniscule black bikini and a pair of sunglasses.

He crossed the stone patio to the deck chair and waited for her to acknowledge his presence.

A minute passed and nothing.

Duke cleared his throat.

"I know you're there. You're blocking my sun. Move, please."

He gritted his teeth and forced a smile. "Miss Love, I'm Duke Morrison from Brotherhood Protectors. Hank Patterson sent me over."

"Fine, fine. You can change into a bathing suit and go for a swim for all I care."

"No, thank you, Miss Love. I'm here to work, not play."

She huffed. "I told Phillip I didn't need a bodyguard here on my own ranch. He doesn't listen."

Duke frowned. "Phillip?"

A frown pulled the woman's lips downward. "My publicity agent."

"If it's all the same to you, I'd like to inspect the house and the security system."

She waved her fingers. "Fine. Do what you have to, just do it out of my sunshine."

He shook his head. "Miss Love, are you sure you should be out in the open?"

She tipped her sunglasses low so that she could stare at him over their rims. "And where else but out in the open would I get sunshine? Seriously, couldn't they have sent me a smarter bodyguard?"

Anger bubbled up inside Duke's chest and rose

in a heated flush up into his face. He had to remind himself he was representing Hank's business. Going off on a customer wasn't the way to get referrals and additional business. He had to resist his urge to lift Miss Love, chair and all, and dump her into the pool. "I'll just have a look at that security system."

"Whatever." She laid back, sunglasses back in place. "Wake me in thirty minutes. I'll need to flip over and tan my back."

He studied her for another few seconds. Yes, she was beautiful, with a body that didn't quit. Long supple legs, with well-defined muscles and taut abs. Her arms were toned, and there wasn't an ounce of flab anywhere on her. She probably paid her personal trainer a small fortune to get her into that kind of shape. Lying down, her breasts weren't nearly as voluptuous as they'd been when she'd flashed them in his face at the bar the night before.

Apparently, she didn't remember him from the Blue Moose. She'd probably been too plastered to remember much of anything.

Good. He'd rather she didn't remember the encounter. If he was lucky, she wouldn't make another pass at him.

"Oh, and Luke?" she said.

"Duke," he corrected automatically.

"Get me a drink on your way back. Jack Daniels on the rocks with a squeeze of lime."

Babysitter, bartender and waiter. Yeah, he'd come a long way from his calling as a highly-skilled warrior.

"Oh, and Luke?" she called, stopping him again.

"Duke," he said, his ire rising by the second.

"Give me a hand up. I feel like taking a dip in the pool."

He reached out his hand, gripped hers and yanked her out of her chair a little harder than he'd intended, his anger fueling his muscles. She slammed into his body, her sunglasses knocked from their perch on her nose.

She stared at him through clear, blue-gray eyes, her mouth opened in a silent O. "Was that necessary?"

"You wanted up," he said. "You're up."

Her pretty brows puckered. "You're a rude man, Luke. I've a mind to fire you."

"My name is Duke. And you'd be lucky to have a mind."

She rolled her eyes. "Luke, Duke. What does it matter? You're blocking my sun again. Move." She planted her hands on his chest and gave him a shove, stronger than he'd anticipated and with a little edge to her voice on the last word.

He stepped backward, remembering too late the pool was right behind him. Before he could stop himself, he fell backward. As he went, he reached for anything to grab hold of. It just so happened to be Miss Love's hand.

Momentum sent him into the water. Quick reflexes and a strong grip brought Miss Love in with him.

He hit the water hard and sank fast.

The woman who'd pushed him thrashed and kicked, hitting him with her heel in his war-damaged knee.

Pain shot through his body, stunning him, making the summer sun dim to gray and finally black.

A moment later, an arm came around him from behind, looped over his shoulder and chest and pulled him to the surface.

As soon as he hit fresh air, he sucked it in, his eyes blinking open. When he realized he was still in the water, he kicked hard and fought the arm holding him.

"Be still, or you'll drown us both," a feminine voice grumbled in his ear.

He leaned back against a warm, soft body, swimming him toward the shallow end of the big pool. When his feet touched the bottom, he stood, getting his bearings and filling his lungs full of life-giving oxygen.

A few steps away in the shallower water, Lena stood, her pretty blond hair plastered to her scalp, her makeup running in black rivulets down her cheeks, her gaze narrowed. "Are you all right?"

For a moment Duke stared at her, trying to comprehend what she'd just asked. Her action, saving him, was so out of character for the diva, she could have been someone else entirely.

Duke wondered if he'd crossed into another dimension where the Lena Love there was actually a nice person, not the spoiled, brat in his own dimension.

"I'm okay," he said, his cheeks heating. His first day on the job as a bodyguard, and his client saved him from drowning. It didn't bode well for the rest of the two weeks.

ANGEL HAD BEEN ACTING full-on diva when she'd managed to send her new bodyguard into the pool. She hadn't expected him to pull her in with him. When she'd surfaced, and he hadn't, she'd panicked for a second. Then the life-saving skills she'd learned when she was a teenaged lifeguard at the neighborhood swimming pool kicked in. She dove down, found Duke and dragged him to the surface, her heart pounding so hard, she could barely breathe. "What happened?"

"Nothing." He waded to the side of the pool and pulled himself up onto the deck.

"Nothing, hell." She followed, determined to get

to the bottom of her bodyguard's near drowning. "You passed out."

"Shit happens," he said, then pulled his T-shirt over his head and wrung it out into the pool. His broad, muscular chest had dozens of little scars, some bigger than others. "I'm fully capable of providing protection for you for the next two weeks." He reached down, offering her a hand to help her out of the water.

She hesitated a moment, and then laid her hand in his.

He pulled her out of the water and up onto the deck without slamming her into his chest like he had earlier.

"Thanks," he said, his tone brusque, his eyes sliding over her from head to toe. "You weren't hurt?"

"No. But I'll have to redo my hair and makeup before the camera crew comes to film her—my home." Even that attempt at her boss's waspishness fell flat of the desired annoying effect.

His gaze raked over her wet head and smeared face. "I think it looks fine. More natural."

Without thinking, Angel raised her hand to her damp cheek.

This bodyguard Phillip had hired had come to the pool with a hint of disgust on his face.

Unfortunately, she wasn't at liberty to be herself. She had to play the part of Lena Love in order to convince anyone who might be lurking in the bushes or on a nearby hillside, watching her. Lena needed the break from her real life and the stalker in order to sober up and get her life back on track. The least Angel could do was to put on a great show to hide the fact she was an imposter.

What she hadn't counted on was her bodyguard blacking out in the pool, requiring her to rescue him. She could bet that wasn't something Lena would have done. Lena would have gotten out of the pool cursing about the insubordinate fool getting her hair wet. She'd have stood on the side of the pool railing about her smeared makeup and saying if he drowned he'd be getting what he deserved for causing her to, Lord forbid, break a fingernail.

"Do you even swim?" she asked.

His brows descended. "Of course."

"Then why were you unconscious?"

"It's not important. Whatever happened won't affect my ability to work."

The man wasn't going to give her anymore information than that.

"Fine." She drew in a deep breath and waved her hand toward the house. "Your sleeping quarters are at the top of the stairs, first door on your right. You might as well change into dry clothes. Oh, and let the chef know you're here and to set another plate at the table."

He started toward the barn.

"Where are you going?" she asked.

Duke stopped and faced her. "To get my duffel bag with my dry clothes. I'll be back in just a minute, at which time I'll bring your drink and, in the process, speak with the chef. Will you require anything else?"

She frowned. "Not yet. I'll let you know when I think of something. And next time, don't be so cocky."

He nodded and left, following the path through the surrounding garden and down the hill to the barn.

The man was not what she'd consider handsome, but he was ruggedly appealing. If she was right, the marks on his chest had been caused by shrapnel. And by the slight limp she'd noted as he walked away, his right leg had issues. Probably caused by whatever had peppered his chest with scars.

Her bodyguard bore further scrutiny, not because his touch had ignited a special electrical charge inside her, but because he wasn't very forthcoming with information about himself.

She knew one thing, though. His name was Duke, and it irritated him when she called him Luke. Her lips quirked on the corners. Maybe she was more like Lena than she cared to admit. She found she liked irritating big, hunky men who thought they knew everything there was to know about the women they protected.

Well, Duke Morrison had another think coming. Lena Love was going to have some fun with the big, sexy bodyguard. Angel's lips curved into a sassy smile. Suddenly, two weeks of ranch living on the Love Land Ranch, didn't sound so boring after all.

CHAPTER 4

DUKE HURRIED to his truck to get the duffel bag he'd left there.

Brandt Lucas caught up with him in front of the barn, half jogging to keep up with Duke, a grin on his handsome face. "I take it you met Miss Love."

"I did," Duke said through gritted teeth.

"She push you in the pool, or did you decide to cool off?"

"I misjudged my footing." And the woman's mean streak. Yeah, he'd witnessed it the previous night, but hadn't imagined she'd stoop to pushing him into the pool fully clothed.

What had him baffled was that she'd saved him from drowning when he'd blacked out. This was a side to Miss Love that was incongruous with everything he'd witnessed and heard about the actress.

For a few moments, she'd been very real and undeniably attractive. Not in the movie star, glossy, superbly-put-together way. She'd almost been a girl-next-door, tough-but-caring woman his mother would have liked.

He liked that version of Lena almost enough to want to stay for the full two weeks. Too bad her mouth had kicked in again after she'd nearly redeemed herself by saving him.

"I don't know why Miss Love needs to hire a bodyguard," Lucas said. "There are plenty of staff members who live here fulltime to look out for her."

"You all have your jobs. I have mine. Perhaps she likes having someone dedicated to securing her well-being." Duke reached his truck, unlocked it and pulled out the duffel bag. When he turned, he almost bumped into Lucas.

"Are you sure that's the only reason she hired you?" The man stood in front of Duke with his arms crossed over his chest, his chin raised, his eyes narrowed.

"What other reason would she have?"

The pimped up cowboy looked down his nose and raked his gaze over Duke. "She usually prefers her lovers to be...better dressed, for one." He sniffed. "You're not her usual type."

Duke almost laughed in the man's face, but

Lucas was blocking his path and irritating him more by the second. "And you're more her type?"

Lucas's smirk was as irritating as his words. "I don't like to kiss and tell, but yes."

Heat burned inside Duke's chest. He clenched his fist around the handles of the duffel bag to keep from throwing it in Lucas's face. Duke's mother would have washed the asshole's mouth out with soap for talking badly about a girl or woman. Though Ms. Love hadn't earned his respect, she was female, and he wouldn't stand by while a prissy man who dressed like a cowboy impugned her character. "Get out of my way."

"Don't say I didn't warn you. Miss Love will use you and discard you like every other male she's brought to her ranch. And if you think pleasuring her will convince her to give you a part in one of her movies, you're going to be disappointed."

"I said, *Get. Out. Of. My. Way.*"

Lucas raised his smooth, manicured hands. "Fine. Have it your way. I'll save my 'I told you so' for when she has you pack up and—"

Duke dropped his bag and plowed his fist into Brandt Lucas's perfect nose.

The man screamed like a girl and fell flat on his ass, getting dirt all over his freshly pressed jeans. Blood spurted from his nose, staining his clean white shirt. "You animal. Why'd you go and do that?"

"I felt threatened," Duke said, his tone flat and bored. "I had to defend myself from your aggression." He fought to keep from laughing.

"Did you have to punch me in my nose?" he whined, tears rolling down his cheeks. "Oh, Lord, I need to see a doctor. No, I need a plastic surgeon. You could have broken it. Oh, my beautiful, perfect nose."

"Don't say I didn't warn you to get out of my way." Duke grabbed his duffel bag, stepped over the man and marched up the slope to the main house, feeling just a little better for having punched someone. Though he felt a little guilty he'd hit someone who was clearly no match for him. It was like kicking a stupid dog. The dog couldn't help he was born stupid. And kicking a dog was just wrong in every way.

But the man had talked trash about his client. For that reason alone, Lucas had deserved Duke's response.

Back through the garden, Duke made his way toward the house, slightly disappointed he didn't see Lena lying in the lounge chair where he'd originally found her. She was nowhere to be seen on the back patio.

Entering through the rear glass door, he stopped to stare at the three-story, cathedral ceiling made of rough-hewn cedar beams arching high over his head.

A bank of windows stretched from the floor all the way up to the impossibly high ceiling, giving a view of the Crazy Mountains most people could never afford in their lifetimes.

Plush leather furniture surrounded a massive stone fireplace, and a thick sheepskin rug lay in front of the hearth. Perfect for a midnight tryst of writhing, naked bodies making love into the early hours of morning.

He could imagine Lena's beautiful body stretched out on the sheepskin, her back arched in the throes of a mind-blowing orgasm.

His groin tightened, and he adjusted his damp jeans. Now was not the time to get a hard-on. Especially for the client. If she lived up to her reputation, she'd have him deliver crackers and cheese to her bed and expect him to share the snack and more.

Before he'd gone for a swim, he'd have said an emphatic *Hell No*.

After she'd saved his ass from certain drowning, his opinion had altered. He saw an entirely different side to the mouthy Miss Love. No, he wasn't naïve enough to think she was cured of her bitchiness in the space of five minutes, but she bore watching. Something wasn't ringing true about the woman.

He headed for the stairs and climbed them one at a time, the injured knee telling him about every step by sending a stab of pain through his leg. The therapist had said he'd have to work the knee daily to get it anywhere near to what it used to be. He'd also said it would never be the same. Duke would have to adjust to a new normal.

Just like his job. He wasn't one of the prestigious Delta Force team anymore. He'd have to adjust to the new normal lifestyle of a rent-a-bodyguard. There was no shame in making a living in an environment where people weren't shooting at him.

Then why was he missing the sound of gunfire and the rush of adrenalin it gave him when he charged into battle?

Most of all, he missed his brothers. Fort Hood seemed a very long way from the Love Land Ranch.

He found the guest room at the top of the stairs, first door on the right, and entered, placing his duffel bag on the floor. The bed was a giant, king-sized, four-poster with thick wooden cannon balls on each corner post. The mattress was covered in a white duvet and piles of feather pillows. A man could lose his women in a bed that size.

Duke unzipped his duffel and fished out a pair of black trousers and a gray polo shirt Hank had given him with the Brotherhood Protectors logo embroidered on the left breast. He figured the outfit would be dressy enough for a bodyguard, without going into the over-the-top stereotype of men dressed in black suits, wearing mirrored sunglasses. He'd ask Miss Love what kind of uniform she expected. Not that he'd necessarily agree to wear it, if it was too hot or too stiff. He needed the ability to run fast (well, as fast as his knee would take him) dive, roll, leap and fight his way out of any situation. Constrictive clothing wasn't conducive to most of those activities.

A door at the side of his room led into an ensuite bathroom with a man-sized shower and a claw-foot tub. Again, he imagined Miss Love bathing naked in the tub, bubbles barely covering the tops of her breasts as she leaned back her head and smiled.

And again, his cock hardened and caused him distress in the still-damp denim.

Trying without much success to put Miss Love's gorgeous body out of his thoughts, he peeled off the wet clothes and slung them over the side of the tub. Then he stepped beneath the showerhead and turned on the cold water, full blast. If he had any hope of chilling his desire, the water would have to be icy cold. His client had a body that could stop a Mack truck. Slim in all the right places, taut enough to bounce a quarter off her belly and smooth, silky skin stretched over firm muscles.

No matter how long he stood under the shower, his desire refused to abate, and her royal pain in the ass wouldn't wait forever for him to get over his hard-on. She'd want that drink he should have gotten her before they both had gone for a swim.

He shut off the water, dried his body and dropped his towel. A knock on the door of the bedroom startled him into grabbing the towel from the floor and wrapping it around his waist.

"Yeah," he said, loud enough whoever was on the other side would hear.

"Phillip and the camera crew are here." Lena said. "Look alive. I need you downstairs ASAP."

The woman sounded more like a drill sergeant than an actress. The firm tone of command lingered in the air and spurred Duke to hurry into his clothes, pull on a dry pair of shoes and head downstairs.

Lena stood by the front entrance, a forced smile stretching her lips across her teeth. Her publicist stood by her side, holding the door as half a dozen men and women entered, passing by Miss Love in their hurry to get inside the famous actress's personal domain.

One by one, the journalists and the crews wandered room by room. Miss Love enlisted the assistance of the housekeeper to explain the layout of the house and the names of each of the suites.

Keeping a close eye on the guests and the camera man, Duke edged closer to Lena, ready to leap in front of her should someone get too close.

At last they worked their way into the master

suite. Everyone was suitably impressed with the beautiful, modern king-size bed with its soft cotton-candy pink comforter.

Lena led the crew into the bathroom, and they all came to an abrupt halt.

"Damn!" Lena cursed. "How the hell did he get in here?"

Duke's adrenaline spiked, and he squeezed between her Publicist and the wall, breaking through to the open interior of the massive master bath.

Lena stood staring at the wall of mirrors, her lips pressed into a thin line.

Written in garish red lipstick were the words:
The predator thrills not in the capture
But in chasing the prey
He revels in the scent of fear

ANGEL HAD to give the author credit for writing that much in lipstick. She'd have given up after the first line.

Despite her flippant outlook on the message, a chill rippled across her skin. The message drawn on Lena's face was playing out. Whoever had it in for Lena was on a roll. She wondered how far he'd take it.

"Everyone out," Duke commanded.

Lena started for the door, but Duke hooked her arm and pulled her against his body.

Electric current zapped through her, heating her where she touched him and spreading that warmth throughout her body. The man was like an igniter switch on a gas burning fireplace. Every time he touched her, her blood burned.

Not a good thing when she needed to keep her secrets and her distance.

Most of the men and women backed out, with the exception of Phillip. The publicity agent's eyes took on an excited glow. He snagged the cameraman as he attempted to fit through the door with the camera on his shoulder. "Where are you going? You need to get a shot of that."

Angel nearly laughed when Duke glared at the two.

"I said get out," Duke said in his lowest, most dangerous and absolutely sexiest voice.

Places farther south inside Angel throbbed to the tone.

"Are you kidding?" Phillip ignored Duke and directed the cameraman. "Get the mirror from this angle." He turned to Lena. "Stand closer to the mirror and look terrified. This is good stuff. It might even make national news."

"Out!" Duke said.

Phillip jumped and finally seemed to hear Duke.

The man really was irritating. Angel didn't know how Lena put up with him.

"You don't understand," Phillip whined. "This is an opportunity to get Lena into the public eye, gain sympathy and show how vulnerable she can be. The studios will eat this shit up."

"You'll have to schedule another show. As long as I'm her bodyguard, this chick's my responsibility." Duke pointed to the door. "Get out, before I throw you out." He stood between Phillip and Angel, his arms crossed over his chest.

Standing behind him, Angel had the best view of all those rippling muscles. As a stunt woman, she was around some pretty ripped dudes. But this bodyguard had alpha magnetism in spades. She could swear he'd been in the military at some time in the recent past. He carried himself with the dignity of a man who'd worn a uniform for his country. Having served herself, she could pick them out in a crowd of civilians.

Angel leaned around him to see if Phillip was actually going to get smart and get out while he still had all of his teeth.

Phillip frowned. "You're supposed to be guarding her, not interfering in her publicity."

"I'm guarding her from you." He grabbed Phillip's arm and dragged him toward the door.

The cameraman scurried out, bumping his big

camera against the doorframe in his hurry to escape the wrath of Duke.

"I'll have a talk with Mr. Patterson about your behavior," Phillip said.

"Do that. In the meantime, don't piss me off." He gave one last shove, sending Phillip stumbling out of the bathroom. Then he slammed the door in the man's face.

Angel couldn't help it, she had to give the man props for taking matters in his own hands and doing what he was being paid to do. "Bravo. I've wanted to do that from the moment he arrived."

Duke turned back, a frown cleaving his forehead. "Then why didn't you?"

She shrugged. "I guess he knows what he's doing. He's the publicist. I'm just the talent." She tipped her head toward the mirror, remembering to play her Lena part. "What a shame."

"What do you mean?"

Her lips twisted. "That was my favorite lipstick." She fought to keep from laughing at the look of disgust on Duke's face.

He shook his head. "Ruining a tube of lipstick is the least of your worries."

"You don't know how hard it is to find a color you simply love." She raised a hand to fluff her hair and stared past the smears on the mirror to study her reflection like Lena would have, every chance she got.

"Sweetheart, that message is a threat."

A shiver of awareness slipped across her skin at his endearment. Not that he'd meant it as such, but on his lips, it sounded kinda sexy. Especially as laced with sarcasm as it was. She wondered what the word would sound like if he spoke it in a low, intimate voice. Another shiver of awareness swept across her and culminated low in her belly. She had to get over the strange attraction she was feeling toward the rugged bodyguard.

"Miss Love, whoever wrote that message there intends to continue his little game. To what end result, I don't know, but it can't be good."

"This place is wired for security. How did he get all the way to my bathroom in the short time between when I greeted my guests and when we arrived back up here?"

"I don't know." He searched the counter and floor.

"What are you doing?" she asked.

"If we could find the tube, we could send it off for latent print analysis. Our trespasser might be in the AFIS system."

"A hardened criminal?" She forced a fake shiver. "Mmm, how deliciously dangerous."

Duke straightened, gripped her arms and stared down into her eyes. "You don't get it. This guy is playing a predatory game with you."

Oh, she got it all right. She was the bait. But

Lena wouldn't know any better. She thought she was invincible. "He's just trying to scare me." She propped a hand on her hip. "I'm not impressed."

"He's a predator. Like a cat playing with his food before he kills it. What if that's his ultimate end game?"

She frowned. "You don't know that."

"True. But I'd rather be safe than sorry. I didn't hire onto this gig to lose my first client because she wouldn't take her own safety seriously."

She dipped her lashes low over her eyes. "That's why I have you, isn't it? I'm paying you to keep me safe."

"If you want me to keep you safe, you have to play by my rules."

"Rules?" She opened her eyes wide and then batted them like she'd seen Lena do on numerous occasions. "Oh, I don't like following rules."

He let go of her and backed away a couple of steps. "Then find yourself another puppet to play with." Duke turned on his heel and started for the door.

Crap. She hadn't wanted him to quit. She was just playing Lena. Apparently, too well. If not Duke as her bodyguard, who else would she get? Better the one she knew than a gamble on someone else.

Angel lunged for him, grabbed his arm and yanked him around. "Wait. Don't go. I'll follow your stupid rules." She rested her hand on his chest.

"Just don't leave me." Leaning up on her toes, she brushed her lips across his. "Please."

He remained stiff and unbending. "My rules?"

She nodded. "Your rules."

A knock sounded on the bathroom door. "Lena?" Phillip said.

Angel released Duke's arm. "Yes, Phillip. What do you want?" she asked, her gaze never wavering from Duke's.

"The camera crew wants you to do a short interview out by the pool. Preferably in one of your designer swimsuits."

She cringed inwardly. Lena might be used to parading around in next to nothing, but Angel liked to keep her clothes on in mixed company. And she'd never expose her entire body unless it was behind closed doors and they were about to make love.

Her core tingled and her gaze slipped down the angular lines of Duke's torso and lower to his narrow hips. Yeah, getting naked with someone like him in private…she could do.

Getting naked in front of a camera and a dozen members of a production team…not no, but hell no.

"An interview by the pool?" She raised her brows in question. "Would that violate your rules?"

"Not so long as I'm nearby," Duke said.

"Then we need to get going." She started to go around him.

He grabbed her wrist and dragged her body up against his. "One other rule."

She looked up into his brown eyes, her heartbeat fluttering against her chest. "Rule?" she repeated, her brain misfiring with the electric currents frying her nerve endings.

"No more of this." He brushed his lips across hers.

Unlike his hard-muscled body, his mouth was soft, his lips full and sensuous. Angel pressed into him, rising up on her toes to get closer to that incredible mouth.

He leaned back just a hair and said, "And never any of this." Duke claimed her lips, crushing his mouth to hers. He pushed his tongue past her teeth.

Angel opened to him and met him halfway, tangling her tongue with his in a frenzied caress that set her entire body on fire with a need she'd never known existed.

His hands swept down her back and cupped her ass.

She raised her hands to caress the back of his neck, deepening the connection, wishing there weren't so many barriers between them. She wanted him...naked...in bed...driving deep inside her.

When at last he set her away, she swayed, her

knees feeling more like jelly than bone. She wiped the back of her hand across her throbbing lips and wondered what had just happened. But then she knew.

She'd just experienced a kiss like none she'd had before. The kind that defined souls and knocked off her socks.

He stared down at her, his eyes narrowed. "Am I perfectly clear?"

"Huh?'

His lips twitched. "The rules?"

She blinked, trying to remember what they'd been talking about. Was he saying they couldn't kiss like they'd just kissed? Inside, her body wailed at the unfairness of such a rule. How could anyone promise not to kiss like that when surely it was as critical to her life as her next breath?

"You're kidding right?" she whispered.

"I never kid," he said. "You're my client. I'm your bodyguard. Anything sexual between us is strictly off limits." His mouth firmed into a straight line, and his eyes narrowed.

Anger jolted through her lust-crazed senses, flushing out all thoughts of kissing this man ever again. She forced a smile to her lips and lifted her chin. "That should be no problem whatsoever on my part." She raised her brows. "Now, if you'll excuse me, my public awaits."

He stepped to the side, allowing her to pass him.

As she did, he leaned close and whispered, "Liar." He cleared his throat. "By the way, they expect you in a swimsuit."

Heat burning her cheeks, Angel marched to Lena's dresser where the actress kept a colorful array of new swimsuits. She grabbed a bright pink one and turned to face Duke, her eyebrows cocked. Then she stepped into the suit bottoms and dragged it up her legs rucking the skirt as she pulled it up over her thighs and buttocks.

Duke's face didn't change, but for the tick in his jaw and the slight narrowing of his eyes.

When she had the bottoms in place, she turned her back and pulled her dress over her head. Slipping her arms into the straps of the suit, she pressed the cups of the bra to her breasts and faced Duke. "Hook me."

Angel presented her back. Yes, she was playing with fire, but the man needed to suffer, too.

He grabbed the straps and hooked them, his knuckles grazing her skin, sending fire shooting through her veins. Her little ploy to make him hot and bothered had backfired.

Forcing a haughty look to her face, she marched out of the bedroom and down the sweeping staircase to the main level.

Angel couldn't get away from him fast enough. The arrogant, conceited man thought he could kiss her like that and remain unaffected. Well to hell with him. She'd show him it was no skin off her nose to ignore him and his ruggedly attractive body. Men! Who needed them?

If her knees were weak, it wasn't because of Duke. If her heart still pounded like a base drum on steroids, maybe she needed to see a doctor. If her core throbbed, aching for more than a single kiss, she'd just have to get out her sex toys and take care of her own needs. She'd be damned if she slept with Duke Morrison. He was strictly O. F. F. limits.

Angel stepped out onto the back patio where the group who'd come to interview Lena was patiently awaiting her reappearance.

She fielded a few pre-approved questions with the canned answers she'd gone over with Phillip. When they'd finished the interview, Phillip handed her a martini, told her to tilt her head toward the sky as if she were enjoying her vacation and the fresh Montana air.

Ready for them to be done, she did what was asked and held the glass in her hand, a martini the last thing on earth she wanted.

As the camera crew filmed, she counted the seconds until she could kick them out and go back to relaxing like she'd been doing before Duke showed up and disturbed her like no other.

She suspected that even if he left the house, he wouldn't leave her mind or senses nearly as quickly.

"One more pose," Phillip said. "With the martini glass for the still shot for the Better Living magazine article."

With a sigh, Angel lifted the glass and pasted a smile on her lips.

The glass exploded in her hand, showering sticky mango martini all over her scantily-clad body.

CHAPTER 5

Duke flew through the air and landed on top of Lena, covering her body with his.

The camera crew scattered.

Phillip hit the deck and crawled beneath a lounger.

Duke wrapped his arms around Lena and rolled off the lounger onto the concrete, taking the brunt of the impact on his right shoulder.

"What are you doing?" Lena asked, writhing in his arms.

"Getting you out of the line of fire." She elbowed him in the gut, and he grunted. "Woman, stop struggling and let me get you out of range."

"Why didn't you just tell me to move? I'm perfectly capable of getting myself wherever it is I need to go."

"Are you getting this?" Phillip yelled to the cameraman.

"Yes, sir," the cameraman responded from behind a brick outdoor kitchen. He squatted down on his haunches, his camera trained on Lena.

"Really?" Duke glared at Phillip. "Miss Love could have been killed and you're still filming?"

"It's great promo," Phillip said. "And the public will love it. I can see the film offers rolling in already."

"Phillip, go to hell," Lena said, and low-crawled like a veteran soldier across the concrete to the door into the house.

Duke followed, using his body as a shield for hers in case the shooter decided to take another shot.

Once through the door, they weren't in the clear until they moved past the huge picture window into another room.

Finally, Lena rose to her feet, a frown denting her forehead, scrapes on her knees and elbows from her crawl across the stone and concrete. "How am I supposed to relax and vacation when some redneck stalker is taking potshots at me?"

Phillip crawled through the back door and stood as soon as he entered the huge living area.

The idiot probably didn't realize he was still silhouetted against the windows.

Duke wasn't going to tell him. As far as he was

concerned, the publicist deserved a bullet to the head. The man was going to get Miss Love killed. "Tell your publicist to take his crew and go away."

"Phillip, take your crew and go back to the hotel." Lena wiped her hands together.

"Okay, okay. We'll leave for now. But we need to come back and get more footage of the outside of the house tomorrow."

"No." Duke shook his head. "You're done. Until we find out who's leaving threatening messages and shooting at Miss Love, no one will be allowed on the estate who doesn't already belong here."

Phillip crossed his arms over his chest. "You can't tell me what to do."

Duke took a step toward the man.

The publicist's eyes widened, and he stepped backward. "Miss Love hired me. She's the only one who can tell me to leave or stay." He turned to Lena.

She narrowed her eyes and let the silence stretch between them. "I didn't agree to an interview in the first place. This was supposed to be a two-week vacation. I can't get any R&R with all of these people around." Then she jerked her thumb over her shoulder. "Go."

Phillip glared at Duke, and then shifted his anger to Lena. "You're only here because of me."

"And I'm only alive because of him." She tilted her head toward Duke. "I plan on staying alive, long after you vacate this house. The sooner you leave with your entourage, the better chance I have, and the better chance Mr. Morrison has of finding the person responsible for the attacks."

Phillip stalked toward her and paused when he came up alongside her. "We'll discuss this later."

"There's nothing to discuss. I'm only here for two weeks. I don't want this fanatic following her —me back to LA, do you?"

Phillip's lips pressed together, and his eyebrows descended. Finally, he responded, "No." He turned to Duke. "Do what you have to do to find out who's doing this."

Duke dipped his head briefly. "That's why I'm here."

The publicist marched through the house and out the front door, ducking low as he exited into the open.

Lena followed the man, closing the door behind him. Then she peeked through the window, without putting herself in view of anyone who could be targeting her.

Duke had to give her credit for staying out of the line of fire. She might be a diva, but she wasn't as stupid as he'd originally pegged her.

The parking area outside the house emptied of all of the vehicles, including the cameraman's van.

Duke walked up beside her. "You did the right thing."

"He only has the best interests of her—my career in mind."

"You won't have a career if you're dead."

She snorted. "Good point." She sighed and glanced around. "What am I supposed to do for the next two weeks if I can't go outside the house? That's not much of a vacation."

"I don't know. Have you tried reading a book?"

She looked around. "I suppose I could."

"Do you happen to know where the security system hub is located? Do you store the recordings?"

She shrugged. "I have no idea. You could ask the foreman. He might know."

"Brandt Lucas?" Duke snorted.

"Oh, right." Her cheeks flushed a soft pink, making her more adorable and vulnerable than the usual spoiled movie star. "How about the assistant foreman?"

Duke nodded. "I'll check with him. For now, I need you to come with me as I search the entire house for any intruders." He pulled his handgun from his side cargo pocket and checked the safety.

Lena frowned. "You think he might be inside?"

"If there is more than one person involved, one could be inside while the other is set up as a sniper."

"And I need to go with you on this tour because…?"

"I can't keep an eye on you and protect you if you're not with me at all times." He captured her gaze. "Are you going to argue with me every step of the way?"

She smiled. "I might. What would be the fun of having a bodyguard if I can't argue with him?"

"As long as you follow my instructions implicitly when the shit hits the fan."

She nodded. "You've got it." Lena waved her hand. "Lead the way."

"You know, you're not half bad when you're not drinking."

She rolled her eyes. "Then I'm not doing my job as a diva. I'll be sure to ratchet up the bitch. Now, shut up and search."

"And she's back." Despite himself, he chuckled at her return to the Lena he expected. Somehow, he couldn't find it in his heart to completely dislike her. Not when he knew how good of a kisser she was, and how sweet her body felt against his. Hell, his lips still tingled from their encounter in the bathroom.

He'd held women to his mother's high standard for a very long time, thus the reason he hadn't married or landed in a permanent relationship. And Lena was not the kind of woman he'd write home about.

But she had a body that didn't quit. If she wasn't his client, he might consider sleeping with her. He could imagine she would be wild in bed.

His groin tightened at the mental image of her naked in his bed, calling out his name as he thrust deep inside her.

Duke gave himself a firm mental shake. He really had to pull himself together, or he'd end up another notch on Lena Love's bedpost.

ANGEL FOLLOWED Duke through the house, getting to know it a little better and getting to know it from the perspective of having to defend herself within its confines.

Someone had entered, trashed the mirror and left without being seen. How could that happen?

Now she followed her bodyguard around, knowing the more she was around him, the more her body responded to his. Sheesh. It wasn't as if she'd gone a long time without sex or anything.

She paused and thought about it. How long had it been? One month, two? She thought back to her last date and bit down hard on her lip. That poor excuse for a date had been over a year ago. She'd been so busy on movie sets and working directly for Lena that she hadn't bothered to have a life of her own. No wonder she was so hot for the bodyguard. She was suffering sexual withdrawals of the worst kind. Trying to think of anything but how she wanted to run her fingers across his bare chest and down the highly defined six pack he carried on his abs, she blurted out, "So, what's your story?"

"What story?" he asked, raising an eyebrow.

"Huh. You're going to play it that way? I'm going to have to pull it out of you?" She nodded. "Fine. Start with how long have you been a bodyguard?"

"Counting today?" he said, tipped his head to the side and squinted into the distance before answering. "Half a day."

"What?" She stepped back. "You aren't even a bodyguard? What's this dude, Hank Patterson, sending out?"

"He hires former military to man his security business."

"So you're former military?" She smirked. Yeah, she'd known it. He had the bearing and the discipline. "What branch?"

"Army."

"MOS?"

He stopped in the middle of the study, and turned toward her. "What do you know about military occupational specialty codes?"

She shrugged and glanced away, her cheeks turning red. "I read." She really had to remember who she was supposed to be. Lena Love wouldn't have a clue what an MOS was. She would barely know there was a difference between the Army, Air Force, Navy and Marines.

"My MOS in the army was 11B, Infantry."

Throwing on her Lena act, she wrinkled her brow and slid her gaze over his muscular form. "Really? I would have thought you were a SEAL or Delta Force like in the movies." She touched his arm.

"SEALs are Navy. Delta Force is the Army's Special Operations Detachment–Delta. Their primary mission is counter-terrorism."

Angel digested his words, a thrill of excitement rippling across her skin. "You say that like you know first-hand."

He nodded. "Maybe I do." He moved through the study, checking beneath the desk, behind curtains and in the small closet. "Right now, we have the mission of searching this house. I take my work seriously."

"You were Delta Force." Angel stared at him with new respect. "Only the best of the best from green beret and rangers are invited to become part of the D-Force team."

He tested the knobs on the French doors before turning to face her. "Yes. I was Delta Force."

"What happened? Why are you working as a bodyguard when you should be countering terrorism?"

He shrugged. "Took one too many hits from

IEDs. The Medical Review Board retired me as of a week ago." Duke's jaw was tight, his lips pressed into a thin line. He hadn't wanted to leave the military. Angel could see it in every groove etched into his face.

She touched his arm. "I'm sorry."

"For what? I got to come home for the first time in years. Some guys aren't that lucky. Some don't come home until they're brought home in a body bag."

Angel could tell leaving the military had been hard for him. She understood. After she'd been injured in a firefight, she too had been processed out, leaving her unit, her brothers and sisters in arms, behind.

To combat her loneliness, she'd returned to her home state of California and had been discovered working at an auto repair shop by a talent agent who'd recognized the startling resemblance she had to the mega-star Lena Love. When he'd discovered she rode a motorcycle and wasn't afraid of fire, taking a punch, or falling through windows, he'd gotten her the gig of playing Lena's stunt woman for the action adventure movies she was known for.

"How does it feel to be back in Montana?" she asked.

He shrugged. "I've barely been outside much to tell. I got in late last night and came straight here after meeting my boss."

Her heart squeezed in her chest. He had to be missing his team. Being an alpha man, he wouldn't let on. Hell, she hadn't, but anyone with eyes would have known her hell-for-leather death-wish wasn't normal for her.

Another thirty minutes searching the premises brought Angel and Duke to the conclusion only the maid, the chef, Angel and Duke were inside the house. Lyle Sorenson, the assistant foreman let them know the security footage was stored on the provider's server, and unless someone had the password to log on, they weren't getting in until the following day during office hours.

The scents of food cooking in the kitchen made Angel's belly rumble. "Supper will be served shortly and Le—I like to dress for dinner." She studied him with a critical eye. "I don't suppose you have anything but jeans with you?"

"I have a pair of trousers and a button-up shirt." His eyes narrowed. "Why?"

"You'll have dinner with me." She lifted her chin, daring him to argue.

Duke shook his head. "That's not necessary. I can wait outside the dining room while you eat."

"You said it yourself. The only way you can protect me is to be with me at all times." She tipped her chin higher and stared down her nose, putting on her full-Lena affect. "I insist." There were advantages to being a pushy, rich bitch. She got her way.

She also presented a target for unwanted attention for the paparazzi and fanatical stalkers. Angel only had to deal with the hassle for two weeks. Lena dealt with it on a daily basis. Yes, she was a pain in the ass, but she never got a minute to herself. That would make Angel nuts, too.

Angel climbed the stairs ahead of Duke and left him at his room to change for dinner. She jumped into the shower, rinsed off the sticky martini and washed her hair.

Quickly blowing it dry, she went to Lena's closet and picked through the dresses, bypassing the leopard prints, loud colors and sheer fabrics, and opting for a simple, floor-length gown of a butter-soft material Angel couldn't name, having never owned anything nearly as nice. The French vanilla, crème-colored dress dropped down over her body like a sensual caress, firing up her blood and making her want to walk back to Duke's room and have him run his hand over the incredible fabric and, of course, every part of her body.

Shaking herself out of the thought, she looked through the jewelry in the built-in drawers of the walk-in closet and selected a pearl necklace and matching earrings.

With her hair down around her shoulders, she glanced at her reflection and gasped. The image wasn't the Angel Carson she knew. What people said about clothes "making the man" was true. She felt like a completely different person. She slipped on a pair of strappy sandals and hurried down the stairs, following the aromas coming from the kitchen.

Duke stood at the bottom of the staircase, dressed in tailored black trousers, a crisp white shirt and black cowboy boots. He'd slicked back his damp dark hair from his forehead and looked like he could model as the Marlboro man. Still rugged and handsome, even in semi-formal attire.

His smoldering gaze swept her length. "Beautiful," he said in that deep tone that made butterflies flutter in her belly. He offered her his arm and led her into the dining room.

Heat rushed up into her cheeks over the compliment. Yeah, he was the bodyguard and he was paid to keep Lena happy, but it still felt good to be noticed and appreciated.

The table had been set for two people, with a candle arrangement providing intimate lighting. Obviously, the chef had assumed Miss Love was entertaining a male guest and probably had plans to seduce the poor schmuck.

Empty wine glasses were set in front of the plates along with napkins and flatware.

Duke pulled out her chair. "Shall we take our seats?"

Angel slipped onto the chair. "What I've had of the chef's meals have been beyond exquisite."

"I'm sure you insist on the best," he said.

Having seen Lena rip a cook a new one for serving a less than stellar hamburger of all things, Angel knew the truth of Duke's statement. "I work hard and make a lot of money. I deserved to spend it the way I like."

"Yes, you do." Duke agreed, taking the seat across from hers.

The maid served the meal one course after another, and was there to collect their empty plates and replace them with the next set without missing a beat.

The meal was a delicious perk of playing Lena Love. The woman really did demand the best from her staff, and they delivered.

Angel ate every last morsel, including the dessert of tiramisu.

Duke shook his head. "How do you stay so thin if you eat that much?" He held up his hands. "Not that I'm judging. It's just that most women eat like birds to keep from gaining so much as an ounce."

"I work it off," Angel said. Granted Lena did pick at her food, but she also worked to keep her body beautiful when she wasn't sucking down the alcohol and drugs.

Duke sat back, holding his cup of coffee in his

hand. "You know my background. What about you? Did you always know you wanted to be an actress?"

Angel nodded. She knew Lena's story, having studied her autobiography to know more about the woman she worked for. "I started out in commercials until my agent set me up for an audition for a movie. Sh—I was eight years old." She shrugged. "The movie hit big and launched my career. I never looked back."

That was about all she knew about Lena's life, other than what she'd witnessed and what the tabloids reported. After a long day of pretending to be the actress, Angel wanted nothing more than to go to Lena's bedroom and be herself behind closed doors.

"I'm tired," Angel said. "It's been a long day. What do you say we call it a night?"

Duke nodded. "I have to admit, I'm pretty tired myself. After driving for the past two days, I could use some real sleep." He rose and held her chair, while she stood and moved away from the table.

Again, he offered his arm.

She took it, knowing that being so close to him was not conducive to sleep. The electric stimulus made her want to strip the clothes off his body and hers and have wild monkey sex in the middle of the living room.

Her best course of action would be to get to her

room as soon as possible, and take another shower. Cold. And go straight to bed.

With a plan in mind, she climbed the stairs and hurried forward, ready to leave Duke behind.

Only he didn't go to his room as she'd expected. "I need to check your room once more before we call it a night."

"Is that necessary?" she asked. "You checked the door and window locks in every room of the house not long ago. Do you think someone could slip in that easily?"

"Locks can be picked," he said.

She rolled her eyes. "Okay. Do your thing. The sooner you're done, the sooner I'll get to sleep."

He made a quick pass through the master suite, checking beneath the bed, the closet and the bathroom where the mirror had been scrubbed clean. "All clear," he reported.

When Duke finally left the room, Angel let out an exasperated sigh and stripped out of the dress. Standing in nothing but a pair of lace panties, she didn't want to get dressed for bed after all. Being near the big D-Force man, she'd learned she was not unaffected by him.

With the man in her thoughts out of the room, the walls seemed farther apart, the cavernous room bigger than her entire first apartment.

Her pulse still hammered against her veins, and she couldn't stay still for long. She needed to get out and run for a couple miles to burn off the calories. Unfortunately, that wouldn't be an option.

Angel paced the length of the room and back several times. Nothing seemed to calm her nerves. A glance at the clock indicated it was getting late. What she really wanted to do was go for a swim.

Surely the shooter wouldn't be out this late at night looking for another opportunity to ruin her day.

She replaced her gorgeous dress with a blue and white LA Dodgers jersey, and then waited another fifteen minutes. The house was quiet, and she didn't hear any movement from the room down the hallway. Angel eased open the door and peered out into the hallway.

A wash of relief warred with disappointment. Duke wasn't in the hallway or on the stairs as she descended to the bottom floor. Knowing she was taking a huge risk, Angel couldn't resist. She needed some space and fresh air to clear her head. Careful not to make a noise, she pushed open the French doors leading out to the pool deck. The lights had been turned off and nothing but the moon lit her way to the water's edge.

Angel stood in the shadows beneath the awning and scanned the vicinity for movement.

Satisfied she was alone, she stripped out of the jersey and walked into the pool in nothing but her panties. Soon she was cleaving through the water, from one end of the pool to the other. The more she pushed herself, the better she felt. By the time she slowed to tread water in the deep end, she was truly tired and ready to go to sleep.

A splash startled her and made her lose her rhythm. She sank beneath the surface and came up spluttering. "What the hell, Duke?" She turned toward the intruder as he surfaced. "Brandt?"

He swam toward her, a smile stretching across his face. "I waited for a long time, but you never sent for me, so I decided to come looking for you."

Angel tried to cover her naked breasts and tread water at the same time, failing miserably with both. "Uh. Brandt, I didn't send for you for a reason. I don't need your services, or whatever you call it."

His brows furrowed, but he didn't slow his advance on her person, moving through the water in an easy breaststroke, his lips curving into a sexy grin. "Playing hard to get? You know that turns me on."

"Seriously, Brandt," she said in her sternest voice. "I'm not in the mood. Don't come any closer.

His grin broadened. "Your mouth is saying no, but your eyes and your body are saying yes."

"Dude, you need an interpreter. My eyes and body are most certainly not saying yes." She gave up covering her breasts and used both arms to swim backward, away from the advancing foreman.

"We usually make love the first night you're back. When you didn't call for me, I thought it was because you were too tired from your trip." He kicked his feet, following her to the deep end. "Why else would you be out here swimming in the nude, if you didn't want to get it on?" He captured her in his arms.

Angel reacted by bringing her knee up sharply, hitting him in the groin.

Brandt swore and curled his body into a ball, but he didn't let go of Angel's arm. "Why'd you go and do that?"

"I told you not to come closer. Now, let go of my arm before I hit you again."

"I don't understand."

Another splash made them both turn toward the latest occupant to the pool.

A dark form shot beneath the surface like a missile from a submarine, a blur of motion, headed straight for Angel and Brandt.

Brandt jerked downward, his head disappearing into the water. With his hand still on Angel's arm, he pulled her under with him.

Angel pried at his fingers, but he managed to get his other hand on her arm and clung to her, in effect, pushing her deeper into the pool.

Her lungs burning, Angel fought, kicked and slammed her hands on his grip, praying he would let go soon, or she'd drown.

CHAPTER 6

Duke had been in the shower when Lena sneaked out of her room. If he hadn't performed one last check before calling it a night, he wouldn't have known until too late. He'd gone into her room with the intention of securing any unlatched windows and asking if she needed anything. When he'd found the bed empty and her missing, his pulse had quickened, and he'd run from the room.

Damn, the woman didn't know what was good for her. She couldn't just go traipsing around her huge house in the middle of the night. Whoever had left the message on her mirror had managed to get inside her security system. If he'd done it once, he could do it again.

Duke had been halfway down the stairs when he'd spotted her through the huge picture windows, swimming laps in the pool. As she'd turned to backstroke in the opposite direction, the moonlight had glinted off her naked breasts.

Duke had been captivated by the perfection of her body, the slim, sleek lines and tight muscles of her arms and legs cleaving through the water. He'd stood transfixed longer than he should have.

Then another figure had dived into the pool and swam toward Lena.

Duke had flown down the steps and across the living area to the back door.

The man had made it across the pool before Duke reached the edge.

And, sweet Jesus, Lena was struggling.

A red flush of rage washed over Duke as he launched himself into the water. Within seconds, he had the perpetrator by the ankle, pulling him under.

Unfortunately, he still had his hands on Lena, dragging her down with him.

Duke climbed up the man's body and hooked his arm around the guy's neck, squeezing hard enough to choke him.

Eventually, the perpetrator released his hold on Lena. She pushed off the bottom and shot to the surface.

Duke swam backward, toward the shallow end where he set the attacker on his own feet and shoved him toward the side. "Get out. And get the hell off the property."

The man who turned to face him was Brandt Lucas.

"Are you insane? You nearly killed me." Brandt coughed, slogging his way through the shallow end to the steps leading out. "I wasn't attacking her. I was trying to make love to her."

Duke shot a glance toward Lena where she clung to the side of the pool, breathing hard. "Is that true?"

"Oh, he was trying," she said, "but I wasn't buying."

When Brandt stood on the deck, he pushed the wet hair off his forehead and sneered at Lena. "You are one crazy bitch. You promised me you'd get me into the movies. I've wasted my time working as your foreman when I could have been working in LA as a model."

Lena shrugged. "Guess you'll have to jumpstart your own career instead of flying on my coattails. Don't let the gate hit you in the backside as you leave."

Brandt grabbed his jeans, jammed his legs into them and dragged them up over his hips. "Should have listened to my agent," he muttered. "Nothing to do out here but listen to the cows bellowing." Finally, he left the poolside, heading toward the barn and the bunkhouse.

Duke raked a hand through his damp hair. "Need a hand getting out of the water?"

She shook her head. "No. No thank you." She had one arm covering her breasts, the other holding onto the side of the pool. "You can go back to bed. I was just finishing up. I'll head inside in just a minute."

His lips quirked. He knew she was naked, and after she'd nearly been mauled by her former foreman, he wasn't letting her off easy. She'd been careless. "I'll wait to make sure you get back to your room safely."

"No need. I can get there on my own."

"Miss Love, you know I can't leave you out here alone," he said, deepening his tone. "Whenever you want to take a swim, you need to let me know. I'll come with you."

"I didn't want to make a big deal of it. I was careful and looked for anyone lurking around, before I got into the water."

Duke's jaw tightened. "But you need someone to watch your back when you can't possibly pay attention. You put yourself at risk." He held out his hand. "Come on inside. You shouldn't be out in the open anyway. The shooter might be watching as we speak."

"I'll take my chances."

Duke walked toward her, the water getting deeper around him. When he couldn't touch the bottom anymore, he swam, moving slowly, giving her the option to get out on her own, or deal with him.

"Don't come any closer," she said.

"I'm getting you out of the water."

"Damn it, Duke! I'm naked. I'm not getting out until you get out first and turn your back."

He chuckled. "I know you're naked. I was watching you from inside the house." He stopped in front of her and he held out his hand. "I won't do anything you don't want me to do. Just come inside where you don't present a target to your stalker." He didn't look down at her breasts, though it took all of his control to resist. Instead, he captured her gaze with his and waited.

She sucked her bottom lip between her teeth, meeting his glance unwaveringly. A moment or two passed. Then she placed her hand in his.

He drew her against his body, treading water with one arm.

Her breasts pressed against his bare chest.

Duke swallowed hard on the groan rising up his throat and said, "Ready?"

"Yes," she said, her voice a breathy whisper. Her thighs bumped into his beneath the water, sending heat blasting through his system straight to his groin.

He swam with her to the shallower water until he could put his feet on the bottom. For some reason, he couldn't force himself to move further.

The moon cast a pale blue glow over her head and shoulders. With her hair lying flat against her scalp, every feature on her face was exposed, from the high cheekbones, to her full, luscious lips.

Perhaps it was the magic of the moonlight that made him bend to touch his mouth to hers. He had to do it, just like he had to breathe.

She met his lips with a soft sigh, leaned into him and wrapped her arms around his neck, her mouth opening to him.

He plunged in, his tongue sliding along hers in an intimate caress. She tasted of tiramisu and coffee. Two of his favorite flavors.

When he had to come up for air, he pressed his temple to hers. "Come on, we need to get inside."

Before she could protest, he swept her naked body into his arms and carried her up the steps, trailing water across the concrete and tile decking.

She reached for the door handle, turned it and let them in the back door.

Duke kicked it shut behind them and let her twist the deadbolt to lock the door.

"You can put me down now."

He shook his head. "Not until I know you're in your room for the night."

She raised her brows. "Have it your way. I'm not that light, and you have a damaged leg. Good luck getting up those stairs."

"No offense, Miss Love, but shut up." He

crossed the smooth, custom oak floors and mounted the stairs, carrying her all the way. He started out fast, but by the time they reached the top of the staircase, Duke was breathing hard, and his leg ached like a motherfucker.

With her arms crossed over her chest and an expression that said, *I told you so,* Lena stared at him. "Uncle?"

He gritted his teeth, dragged in a deep breath and then strode down the hall. At her bedroom, he kicked open the door, entered the huge room and dumped her ass on the king-sized bed.

"Hey! That wasn't very nice." She righted herself and pulled the comforter over her nakedness. "You, Mr. Morrison, are no gentleman."

"And you, Miss Love, are no lady. Didn't your mother teach you to wear a swimsuit when you go swimming out in the open?"

"It's my place. I can walk around stark naked wherever the hell I please." She tilted back her head and stared down her nose at him. "Besides, a polite gentleman would have looked away."

"Since we've already established that I'm no gentleman, it's a moot point." He strode to the windows, checked the locks, double-checked the bathroom and ducked to glance under her bed.

A slim, bare foot shot out hitting him in the shoulder, knocking him backward.

He grabbed the ankle attached to the foot as he

went down, dragging her off the bed. They landed in a tangled heap on the sheepskin rug.

Lena tried to scramble out of reach.

Duke wasn't having any of it. "Prepare to reap what you sew." He flipped her onto her back on the rug, straddled her hips and pinned her wrists high above her head. Then he stared down at her flushed face.

"I don't think pinning your client to the floor is in your job description." She wiggled beneath him, igniting his desire for this mess of a woman.

"I'm guarding your body." His gaze slipped lower. "And since you seem to enjoy strutting around in your birthday suit, I assume you have no problem with your bodyguard seeing you nude." His glance slipped to the breasts he'd seen last night, flashed fully in his face. Only this time, there was something different. On her left breast, just below the nipple was a tattoo of a heart surrounded by two doves in flight.

He froze, studying the tattoo.

"Hey, you can quit staring now," she said, her cheeks turning redder by the minute. She arched her back in an attempt to dislodge him.

Still holding her wrists with one of his hands, he pointed at the mark. "This tattoo, when did you get it?"

She stopped struggling. "When I was eighteen. The year my parents died."

For a moment, her words hung in the air, as if they didn't quite belong anywhere. Then it all came crashing down around Duke.

He glared down at her. "Who the hell are you?"

Her eyes widened as she stared up at him. "Wh-what do you mean? I'm Lena Love. Who else would I be?" Her gaze slipped to the corner of the room.

"The woman in the bar who flashed me last night was Lena Love. She didn't have a tattoo on her breasts. You, however, do."

She set her jaw in a tight line. "Get off of me."

Duke shook his head. "Not until you tell me what the hell is going on."

ANGEL COULD TELL by the dark look in Duke's eyes he wasn't going to buy any more of her bullshit.

"I'm Lena Love, and I'm ordering you to let go of me."

He shook his head. "Nope. Try again."

She fought to free her wrists, finally giving up. "Fine. Let me up, and I'll tell you what you want to know."

For a long moment, he continued to hold her wrists above her head. Then he abruptly released them and rose to his feet.

Angel covered her breasts with her hands, glad she at least still wore panties. Though, even with everything covered, she felt completely exposed to his all-seeing gaze.

He reached a hand down to her.

She ignored it, rolled to her side and pushed to a standing position. With her back to him, she crossed to a dresser, pulled out a leopard print nightgown, threw it down in disgust and found a plain gray T-shirt. Pulling it over her head, she turned to confront her bodyguard.

"Come with me." She led the way into the bathroom with its bright white walls, brushed chrome fixtures and muted lighting

Once she closed the door behind him, she turned on the water in the shower. "Just in case anyone is listening in or recording our conversation," she explained, even though he hadn't asked. Nervous now, she tugged at the hem of the T-shirt, noticing too late that her nipples poked into the fabric making little tents.

"Start talking," Duke ordered.

"I will. I will. Keep your britches on." She turned away and pushed her wet hair out of her face. "Last night when Lena was at the bar, she consumed too much alcohol and did things she would never do sober." At least Angel hoped she wouldn't flash someone when she wasn't high or drunk. The truth was that Lena was a loose cannon, on a one-way trip to cratering her career if she didn't get sober. "We found her in the ladies' room passed out on the floor. Someone had written a message on her face in indelible ink."

"What was the message?"

Bitch. I'm going to make you pay."

Duke shook his head. "Did you ever consider that information might be important to a bodyguard?"

"I suppose it would have been nice to know."

"So, who are you?"

"I'm Lena's stunt woman and body double."

Duke snapped his fingers impatiently. "Do you have your own name?"

"Angel Carson."

"Background."

"Prior military, currently a stunt woman."

"Branch and specialty?"

"Army Ranger."

"Seriously?" He stared at her, as if seeing her for the first time. "Not many women have made it through Ranger training."

"I know. I was in the second class that allowed female trainees."

"Why did you get out of the Army?"

"Not because I wanted to." She glanced away. "TBI – Traumatic Brain Injury." She touched a finger to her head. "My team got caught in an explosion. I survived, but the impact scrambled my brain enough the Medical Review Board processed me out."

"And you thought being a stunt woman would improve your brain injury?"

Angel shrugged. "What else was I fit for? I trained to go into dangerous situations, to shoot and be shot at."

"How did they know you had a TBI?"

She snorted. "I was in a coma for a week. When I came to, I had temporary amnesia and situational amnesia of the attack."

"That's normal. The brain protects you from reliving the trauma."

"Not completely. I had terrible nightmares, but couldn't remember them when I woke. At first my sense of taste and smell were off. I had dizzy spells and really bad headaches. Those symptoms faded as time passed."

"I'm sorry you had to go through all of that."

"I was sorry I lost my team, my career and everything I knew." She shrugged. Three years had passed since then.

"How did you land a job as a stunt woman?"

She gave a short smile. "It's one of those Hollywood stories you always hear about. A scout spotted me at an oil change place. The rest, you could say, is history."

"Where is the real Lena Love?"

"Phillip was supposed to get her checked into a rehab facility to dry her out and clean up her face. Meanwhile, I'm the bait for her attacker." She drew in a deep breath, glad to get all of that off her chest. "I never was a good liar. I'm glad you know. But you can't tell anyone. In order for Lena to get the privacy she needs, I have to put on a convincing act as the real Hollywood diva." She gave him a crooked smile. "So, was I convincing?"

Duke chuckled. "At first, yes. But I think I knew deep down, you weren't the same woman from last night. For one, Lena Love would never have pulled me out of the pool. She probably would have let me drown before she called for help."

Angel nodded, her lips twisting into a wry grin. "You're probably right."

"The question is, where do we go from here?"

"Nowhere," Angel said. "I'm here for the remainder of the two weeks, making the staff nuts and being a pain in the ass to anyone and everyone with whom I come in contact."

"I don't like that you're putting yourself up as the target. The bullet that hit your martini glass this evening could easily have hit you instead."

She nodded. The thought had occurred to her, and she hadn't been all that happy about it.

"Who has Lena pissed off enough to want to cause her a whole lot of grief and possibly even kill her?"

"Hell, who hasn't she pissed off?" Angel sighed. "The possibilities could be too many to calculate."

"Any rivals vying for the same parts?"

"She is up for a really big part in a movie. Phillip has been waiting on pins and needles for the call."

"Who else is being considered for that part?"

"You'll have to ask Phillip. He knows all of the ins and outs, and the actresses and actors who are anybody in Hollywood." Angel sighed. "I'm just the stunt woman. Nobody of consequence in the grand scheme of the big studios."

"Except you look like Lena Love, which has put you in the unlucky position of being the decoy to draw out a potential killer." Duke frowned. "We have to find this person before he makes good on thinning the talent pool."

"We don't know he's out to kill Lena." Angel perched on the edge of the bed and tugged at the T-shirt's hem.

"No, but that bullet today made it an entirely different game. One we want to win. If we're serious about luring him out into the open, we need to take the game to a new level."

Angel frowned. "And how do we do that?"

"Ever been camping in Montana?"

Her frown deepened. "No. Sounds cold and uncomfortable."

"If we stay here at the house, you're nothing but a sitting duck. If we lead him up into the hills, we can switch the hunted to the hunters."

A slow grin spread across Angel's face. "I like the way you think."

"Yeah?" He chucked a finger beneath her chin. "I like the way your nipples poke at your T-shirt. I suggest you go to bed and get some sleep. Tomorrow we head into the mountains."

She frowned. "Hey, you're not supposed to be so obvious about your lascivious observations."

He gave her a lopsided grin. "Yeah, well we've already established I'm no gentleman."

Angel's lips twisted. "Your mother would be so proud."

"Leave my mother out of this."

She rose from the bed and poked a finger into his chest. "Leave my nipples out of this." Angel jutted out her chest, parading her pointy breasts as she headed for the door. When she reached it, she flung it open and tipped her head. "Goodnight, bodyguard."

"Goodnight…Lena." As he passed her, he leaned close, captured her head in the palm of his hand and whispered, "Angel fits you so much better."

Her body quivered. "Just so you know, my teammates called me the Angel of Death." She shot him a challenging glance.

"I can see it. You wouldn't be where you are today, if you were any other way."

Angel frowned.

Duke shook his head. "I meant that in the best, strongest way." With his hand still cupping her head, he bent and captured her lips with his. When he raised his head again, he smiled that sexy smile that turned her knees to melted butter. "Oh," he said, his voice deep and husky. "I'm sleeping in your room, tonight."

She had been leaning toward him, her entire body drawn to him like a moth to a flame, when his words sank in. She jerked back. "Like hell you are."

He patted her cheek like a parent pats a child's. "Get used to it. We're going to be spending a lot of time together over the next couple of days. Or however long it takes to flush out your stalker."

Her pulse thundered through her veins, and her palms grew moist, along with another place farther south. How was she going to resist this man if he insisted on being right beside her? Day and night? A normal, sexually deprived woman could only take so much before she conceded defeat and begged to join the other side.

CHAPTER 7

DUKE LAY on the chaise lounge in Lena Love's bedroom, trying not to think about the tattoo on Angel's breast and the fact that, since she was a decoy for Lena, she really wasn't his client. Lena was.

Which meant the separation between client and bodyguard didn't apply to him and Angel. Why that gave him a sense of joy, he didn't know.

He really should consider Angel off limits as well. She wasn't his type. Nothing about her was like his age-old image of the perfect woman. She was as different from his mother as night from day.

His mother had stayed home and raised her sons, helped with homework, sewed, cooked cleaned and made their lives better with her loving, nurturing nature.

Despite her name, Angel didn't strike Duke as the kind of woman who could sew curtains to frame a window, or sauté onions and make a roast that would melt in his mouth. She had a smart mouth and a hard knee that hit with a wicked determination to end an attack before it got ugly. She had proven herself in her training as an elite Army Ranger and then she'd faced combat head-on. He'd never met a woman who'd willingly walked into a war-torn area, knowing she could get killed or maimed, and still function without launching herself into a fit of hysterics.

The woman probably didn't know a saucepan from a skillet. Cook a roast? Probably not.

But he had the feeling if he handed her a rifle, she'd know how to disassemble and assemble it in under a minute. And he'd bet his favorite nine-millimeter pistol she was an expert marksman. The Army Rangers only graduated the best of the best. They didn't cut the women any slack to fill a quota. If anything, they had to work harder than the men to prove themselves.

"Are you asleep," her voice said in the dark.

"No," he answered.

"I've laid on that lounge. It's not very comfortable."

"No. It's not." He rolled onto his back and nearly fell off the narrow chaise that was barely big enough to hold him.

A long pause stretched between them.

"It's ridiculous for you to sleep there when this bed is sufficiently large enough for two people. We would never touch each other."

That's where she might be wrong. If Duke slept in that bed with her, he wouldn't have the ability to resist touching her. "I'll sleep here."

Silence stretched between them.

"Seriously, you should take the other side of this bed. I'll feel bad if you don't get any rest when we're about to go days without sleep."

"I'm not likely to get any sleep if you keep talking," he said into the darkness.

She snorted. "See if I try to be nice again."

"I know it's a stretch."

"Damn right it is."

"Geez woman, if I move to the bed, I can't guarantee I won't touch you." There, if she didn't already know he was attracted to her in a big way, she did now.

"I said we wouldn't *have* to touch." Her little pause lengthened. "Unless we wanted to," she said, her voice fading into the shadows.

"Don't ask, unless you really mean it. Once I've tasted the honey, I won't be able leave the hive."

Angel burst out laughing. "You didn't just liken my lady parts to a beehive, did you?"

A smile played at Duke's lips. "I did." He pushed to his feet and crossed the room to where she lay in

Lena's big bed, covered in that damned cotton-candy-pink comforter.

Still chuckling, she shook her head. "I'm sorry, but that's about the most unromantic thing a man has ever said to me."

He tipped his head to the side. "Scoot."

She moved over to make it easy for him to slide onto the mattress.

"How's this." He lay on his side and leaned up on one elbow. "Your lips are as soft as my dog's belly."

"Not even close," she said, staring up at him in the little bit of moonlight streaming through the window.

"No?" He pushed a strand of her hair back behind her ear. "I really loved my dog."

"You're going to have to do better if you want to stay with me tonight."

"Mmm, I know just what to say."

She shook her head. "I'm almost afraid to ask, but here goes. What would you say?"

"I knew there was something different about you this morning. In many ways, you look very much like Lena, but you're not like her at all. I couldn't put my finger on it until just now. Where Lena is all about Lena, you care about others." He tapped her chest. "You have a heart. Otherwise, you wouldn't have saved me from drowning and you wouldn't have agreed to be the bait to draw out her stalker."

"What else have I got to do in my life?" she asked, her voice not much more than a whisper. "I'm not married. I don't have kids. I don't even have an impressive career."

"You have all of your life to live the way you want. And you deserve to make it happy."

"Life's not the same when you have no one to share it." She touched her fingers to his bare chest.

"You need to stop living Lena's life and make one of your own."

"Now, that's pretty romantic," she said, cupping his cheek. She leaned close and pressed her lips to one of his little, hard brown nipples. "I think you might have potential."

"For what?"

"Well, not as a gentleman, but then I never stated a preference for gentlemen. I kind of like my men to be a little more rugged."

"I can be rugged," he leaned over her and nibbled on her earlobe, nipping just a little harder to make his point.

"Ow." She raised her hand to her ear and laughed. "But gentle when he needs to be."

He slipped his hand along her arm and down to her waist, stopping to balance on her hip. "How am I doing?"

"I don't know. There appears to be too much getting in the way of this lesson in what this lady wants and what you have to offer."

"Like?"

She slid her hand into the waistband of his boxer shorts and snapped the elastic. "Getting the idea, cowboy?"

"I think so. I might be a grunt, but I can be taught." He slipped her T-shirt over her head and tossed it to the floor.

She helped shove his boxers down over his hips and thighs, her fingers trailing across his skin, making him crazy with need. This slow, steady, getting-to-know-you dance they had started couldn't get moving fast enough. He longed to take her, to slide into her warm, slick wetness. But first, he wanted her to reach the level of insanity she was inspiring in him.

He slid a finger along the smooth line of her jaw and down the long, slender column of her neck. Moving lower, he skimmed the rounded swell of her breasts, stopping to tweak the nipple and circle the tattoo. "What does the tattoo stand for?"

"The kind of love that brings two people together for the rest of their lives. The kind of love my parents have for each other."

"That's beautiful." He kissed the bead of her nipple, and then flicked it with the tip of his tongue. "Like you."

"Wow," she said, her words catching on her indrawn breath. "Now, you're getting the idea."

"I told you, I can be taught. But it's easy when

the recipient inspires me." He circled her nipple several times before sucking it into his mouth and pulling hard.

He was quickly falling into her, without a care as to how to disengage and walk away when the two weeks were up, or the stalker was found and carted off to jail.

Duke had no intention of leaving Montana any time soon. Living in LA was not even a consideration. But then, he and Angel had only just met. They'd known each other for such a short amount of time. Dreaming of a future with her would be insane.

Then why was he thinking about how many more times he'd like to make love to this woman? That implied a future that couldn't be.

ANGEL CLOSED HER EYES, pretending she and Duke weren't in Lena Love's bed but on some tropical island in the middle of the ocean, away from everything that could get in the way of this moment. She ran her hand across his rock-hard shoulder and down over his chest. "What about you?"

He brushed the tip of her nose with his lips and then took her mouth in a long, soul-tugging kiss that left her breathing hard and wanting so much more.

"What about me?" he asked, his fingers feathering over her hip and sliding down to the tuft of hair over her sex.

"What made—" her words caught in her lungs as he parted her folds and flicked the nubbin between, "—you want to be Delta-Force." There, she'd gotten it out, now she could draw in another breath.

He flicked her again, and her insides tensed, squeezing her lungs, her core, her senses. She couldn't think past what he was doing to her down there.

"I love my country. I like being all I can be, and Delta Force was that."

"Were you processed out for medical reasons, too?" He hit the right spot, and she gasped. "There. Oh, sweet Jesus. There!" She arched her back off the bed.

Duke's hand followed, cupping her sex until she settled, and then he resumed teasing that bundle of nerves to a fever of excitement.

"Yes. Medically retired," he answered.

"Leg?" She managed to push the word from her lungs as another wave of sensations rocked her. Angel drew her knees up and let them fall to the side.

"Leg."

"Does it keep you from..." God, he flicked her there again. She was so close to a full-on orgasm she couldn't finish her sentence. Hell, she couldn't remember what she had been saying.

"Keep me from making love to you?" He chuckled. "Oh, hell no."

"Good. Because I want you."

"Then show me how much." He parted her legs and lay down between them, skimming a trail of kisses and nips down her abdomen to the place that was already so sensitized she was almost afraid she'd come apart into a million pieces if he touched her there with his tongue.

And then he did.

Angel rocketed to the heavens, her body exploding with sensations, until she couldn't remember what was earth and what was sky. She rode the wave through to the very end, her hips pumping, her hands buried in his hair, fingers flexing into his scalp.

When she came back to the earth long enough to breathe, she tugged on a handful of his hair. "Now. Inside me. Hurry."

He crawled up her body and pressed his cock to her entrance, and then stopped.

"Holy crap, Duke," she wailed. "Why are you stopping now?"

He grinned, though his mouth appeared strained as if he could barely hold back. "Protection?"

"Fuck!" She slammed her fist against the

mattress. They couldn't get to the door and not go in. Then she thought about Lena. "She has got to have a stock of condoms. Check the nightstand."

Duke leaned over, pulled open the top drawer of the nightstand and laughed. "You were right. She's got everything. A year's supply of condoms, sex toys, lubricant and even several varieties of whips."

"Stop talking," Angel commanded. "Am I the only one turned on here?"

He selected a condom, his face splitting into a grin. "Impatient much?"

"Fuck you." She snatched the package from his hand, tore it open and rolled the item over his rock-hard cock. "Now, get busy. I'm riding an orgasm I don't ever want to stop."

"Mmm." He bent to take her mouth with his, sucking her bottom lip between his teeth where he bit down softly before releasing it. "You're so romantic when you curse like a sailor."

"Like a Ranger. Get it right." She clasped his ass in her hands, done with the chatter and ready to take him all the way home.

Once again, he positioned himself at her entrance and gently dipped in.

Her muscles contracted, as if to pull him deeper inside her channel. Past patience, and so hot she could spontaneously combust, Angel grabbed his buttocks and slammed him home.

"Oh, sweet Jesus. Now we're headed in the right direction."

Duke slid out, the movement excruciatingly slow.

Angel wrapped her legs around his waist and dug her heels into his backside, wanting him inside again, filling her to full and fucking her like there was no tomorrow.

Finally getting the hint, Duke moved in an out, increasing the pace and the intensity until he was pounding, hard and fast.

"Yes!" Angel yelled.

She dropped her heels to the mattress and dug in, lifting her hips to meet him thrust for thrust.

His body tensed, his jaw hardened and he slammed into her one last time, driving deep and holding there, his cock pulsing against the walls of her channel.

Angel came, her sex convulsing around his, her body shaking with the power of her release.

A minute passed, maybe two, before Duke lay down on her, wrapped his arms around her and rolled her and him onto their sides without disturbing their intimate connection.

Angel lay spent, her heartbeat slowly returning to normal. "Wow," she said when she could get enough breath to form a word.

"Wow, yourself," Duke managed. "I didn't expect

sex with Lena Love could rock my world so completely." He winked.

"Hey. Lena's got nothing on me."

"Damn right. You're one in a million."

She snorted. "Remember that."

"I'm not likely to forget for a very long time." He cupped her cheek and stared deep into her eyes.

Angel's thoughts clarified in that instant and shook her even more than the most incredible orgasm she'd ever experienced.

Her gut bunched into a tight knot.

I could fall for this guy. I mean, really fall.

Hard.

CHAPTER 8

DUKE PACKED a shirt and a pair of jeans into a backpack, and then threw in a handful of condoms he'd grabbed from the stash in Lena's nightstand. Not that they'd have time or the opportunity to make love in the mountains. But he could never be too prepared.

"Look at this." Angel carried a lightweight laptop into the room and set it on the bed beside his backpack. "Lena Love dumped Myles Crain a week ago after the media got hold of some pictures of his trophy hunts in Africa." She scrolled through several photos of a handsome man in khaki slacks and shirt, standing beside the carcass of a slain elephant. The next was Myles Crain smiling for the camera beside a dead giraffe, its neck folded over neatly to fit in the picture. The last one was of Myles and a lion. He held the head up, the lion's jaw had dropped open, exposing razor sharp teeth that had been no match for the hunter's long-distance rifle.

"He's a real sweetheart, isn't he?" Duke commented. "Seems like the kind of guy Lena would go for. One who likes to shoot caged animals."

"That's just it. She didn't want to dump him." Angel closed the laptop. "I called Phillip to get the story. He told her she had to dump him. Myles was getting so much bad publicity, it threatened to impact her career. If she didn't dump him, he'd bring her down with him." Angel's lips twisted. "She dumped him publicly, through a television interview on a major talk show. Phillip said Myles was livid. He even called Phillip and threatened to kill him."

"A regular Prince Charming and a potential suspect."

Her brows twisted. "Another thing I found out about him that might put a damper on our trip into the mountains…"

"What? He likes to shoot women holding martini glasses?"

"No. He's big into predator games. He belongs to a league of hunters who pay men to be human prey."

"Like laser tag?" Duke's stomach knotted.

"Like laser tag on steroids. It's on a much

grander scale. The course is over a thousand acres. The hunters have to track the individuals. The runners who stay 'alive' the longest are paid top dollar."

"So he's had some experience tracking humans as well as animals in a pen." Duke laid out an array of weapons on the comforter. "I'm liking this guy more and more." He held up a military-grade rifle. "Know how to use one of these?"

She lifted the weapon, pulled back the bolt, peered inside, and then closed it again. "Of course. It's an M4A1 with a SOPMOD upgrade. We used these in my unit. Pretty damned accurate." She hefted it in her arms. "This one mine?"

He nodded. "And this." Duke handed her an M9 Beretta and holster with a belt.

"Where did you get all of this?"

"I have my conceal carry license."

She snorted. "This is enough stuff to supply an army."

"My new boss has connections."

Angel shook her head. "We're up against one man."

"And you've been in combat. One man can cause a lot of damage."

She nodded, her lips pressing into a thin line. "You're right." Squaring her shoulders, she dipped into the duffel bag he was loading with all of the guns and ammo. "Good, the magazines are loaded."

Duke grinned. "Not much good if they aren't."

"When are we leaving?"

"In ten minutes. I spoke with the foreman about hunting cabins on the ranch."

"The foreman?" Angel cocked her brows.

"Not Brandt Lucas. He was a figurehead."

"More likely a Lena fuckbuddy," Angel commented.

"He's long gone. Packed his shit and left last night."

Angel shivered. "Good riddance."

"Sorenson said there's a hunting cabin on a peak a couple of miles into the mountains. He gave me the general directions. We should be able to get there in an hour or two."

"I'm packed and ready when you are. I'll be in the kitchen loading some staples in case we're there for longer than a day or two."

"I'll be down in a couple of minutes. Stay away from the windows. Don't present a target."

She shook her head. "I'm not a newb."

"Yeah, but you haven't been in combat for several years." He grabbed her arm, pulled her against him and kissed her lips. "Humor me, will you?"

She smiled. "Okay. But only because I like your weapons." With a wink, she turned and left the room.

Duke called Hank Patterson and let him know

what they'd discovered about Lena's ex-boyfriend and what had been going on since Duke had taken on the assignment as Lena's bodyguard.

"It's a good thing she has you to look out for her," Hank said. "Shooting a glass out of her hand is far too close for comfort."

"Yeah, well, I have a plan." Duke laid out his plan to lure the stalker away from the ranch and up into the mountains.

"Are you sure you want to do it that way?" Hank asked. "I can bring in my other agents from their current assignments to back you. But you'd have to give me at least a day. I can come with you now and we can have the others join us when they get in."

"I'm afraid if I take an army up into the mountains, our stalker won't come out of hiding." He glanced at the arsenal of weaponry he was taking with him. Knowing Angel could handle a gun as well as he could, made it easier for him to say, "I'm pretty confident I can manage this on my own." He wouldn't be on his own with the real liability that was Lena. Angel would be a member of his team, an asset to the upcoming fight.

"I can't say that I like the idea of you and Miss Love going up into the mountains without more support."

"Remember, I'm from Montana. I know my way around the mountains."

"You might know your way around, but does Miss Love?"

"I'll take care of her." And he would. But she'd also be fully capable of taking care of herself.

Hank sighed. "Okay. I'll give you two days, and then I'm coming up after you."

"Fair enough," Duke agreed. "I hope it won't take two days. I'm aiming to be back at Love Land after only a night."

"I admire your conviction. I just hope it's not misplaced."

"Give me two days."

"Okay." Hank ended the call.

Duke tossed the phone on the bed and sifted through the magazines and pouches.

When his cellphone rang, he spent a few seconds looking for it amid the magazines, ammunition and pouches scattered across the bed. When he found it, he noticed the caller ID and hit the talk button. "Hey, Rider. You guys really must be missing me."

"Not at all. We're just jealous as hell that you're having all the fun in Montana without us."

Duke snorted. "Fun. Right."

Rider's tone grew serious. "What's happening?"

"You could say I'm missing my brothers about now."

"Protecting a movie star more than you can handle?"

"She's got a psycho hunter after her. He's only been playing with her to begin with, but he took a warning shot at her yesterday."

"Damn," Rider said. "And here we all thought bodyguarding was a boondoggle."

"Me too, until it got too close to home, and a lot more dangerous."

"Well, don't tell the guys I was the one to blow the surprise, but me, Blaze and a couple others packed our fishing gear and chartered a plane leaving today."

"For?"

"Eagle Rock, Montana."

A wave of relief washed over Duke. He'd have his team as backup if the shit hit the fan. "How soon will you be here?"

"We leave in fifteen minutes," Rider said. "Flight time is under five hours. Think you can hold out until we get there?"

"I think so. I told my boss I didn't need help, but you can never have too many Deltas on a mission."

Rider chuckled. "Got that right."

"We're heading into the mountains to see if we can force his hand."

"Send us the coordinates. We'll be there."

"Roger." For the first time since he'd left Fort Hood, Texas, he felt like he had a mission. Something to fight for. "Hopefully, by the time the team gets here, it'll be that cake walk you mentioned and we'll get in some fly fishing."

"Yeah." Rider paused. "Stay safe, buddy."

"Will do."

If all worked out as planned, they'd lead the stalker into the woods, turn the game on him and the predator would become the prey.

Between a former Army Ranger and a Delta Force soldier, they should be able to flush out the bad guy and give him a little of his own medicine. His hunting days would soon be over.

And if all else failed, the cavalry was on its way for some fly fishing, and other duties as required.

"I HAVE to admit I feel a little better wearing body armor," Angel said softly, so only Duke could hear. As she stood in front of the barn, she adjusted the Kevlar vest beneath the oversized blouse she'd found in Lena's closet. She glanced around. "What vehicle are we taking?"

Lyle, the recently promoted ranch foreman led two horses out of the barn and handed the reins of a big black one to Duke.

As he led the bay toward Angel, she held up her hands, shaking her head. "I'm not riding that."

"Why not?"

Angel bit her lip, about to say it was in her contract that she didn't have to do any stunts requiring her to ride a horse. But even though she'd told Duke who she was, no one but Phillip knew she wasn't the real Lena. And Lena rode horses. Damn. "I just don't feel like riding a horse today." She glanced around. "Don't we have four-wheelers or something?"

"Some of the trails up to the cabin are really narrow. A horse has a better chance of getting around," Lyle said. "Miss Love, you know you feel safer riding horses than four-wheelers. Besides, it's been weeks since you've taken Hollywood for a ride."

The horse danced away from Angel. Though humans couldn't tell the difference between Angel and Lena, the horse obviously smelled a difference. It was probably the fear Angel was sweating out of every freakin' pore.

Without making a big fuss and revealing her lack of horse-riding skills, Angel gritted her teeth and stuck her foot in the stirrup.

The horse danced away again.

Angel held onto the side of the saddle, hopping along beside the horse.

"Don't know what's gotten into that animal." Lyle held onto the bridle and steadied the beast while Angel mounted, swinging her leg over the top of the saddle and landing with a jarring thump on her ass.

Sweet Jesus, I'm going to die!

Forcing a smile to her face, she said, "Let's ride!" If her voice was shaky and her grip on the reins wasn't right, well, fuck it. She was doing what she'd always sworn she wouldn't—riding a goddamn horse!

Her legs cinched around the horse's belly.

As soon as Lyle released the bridle, Hollywood danced sideways.

Angel bit down hard on her tongue to keep from crying out. Her feet flapped in the stirrups, and her heels touched the horse's flanks.

Hollywood leaped toward the gate, nearly leaving Angel behind.

By the grace of God and her hold on the saddle horn, she barely managed to remain in the saddle.

Hollywood stopped at the gate and waited for Lyle to open it.

Lyle stared up at the horse and scratched his head. "Don't know what's wrong with that horse. He never acts this way around you."

"I've been a little off kilter. Maybe he senses it," Angel bit out between her gritted teeth. "We'll work the kinks out on the trail. See you in a couple of days." She lifted her hand briefly in a little wave.

"Enjoy your stay in the cabin. I was up there a week ago. It's all set up with canned goods and firewood."

"Thank you, Lyle," Angel said, before she remembered Lena wouldn't have been as nice.

Duke rode up beside her, his horse stopping close enough Duke's leg touched Angel's.

A flash of desire raced through her at his nearness.

"Ready?" he asked.

Oh, yeah. She was ready to go back up to Lena's bed and make a repeat performance of last night. She sighed. Alas, they had a dangerous job to do. Hopefully, her stalker was watching and already planning to follow them up into the mountains. "Ready as I'll ever be," she said, her eyes narrowed. She was ready to take out the bastard bent on making Lena's life hell and ending it in a fantasy hunt to the kill.

Angel called bullshit on that. She and Duke would turn the tables on the bastard and bring him down.

DUKE LED THE WAY, following the directions Lyle had given, along with the GPS device he'd brought in his gear.

After they had ridden out of sight of the barn and house, he'd slowed for Angel, snapped a lead rope onto Hollywood's bridal and led the animal behind his horse.

"You didn't tell me you couldn't ride."

"It never occurred to me that we'd take horses up in the mountains."

"Sweetheart, we're on a ranch…with horses and cattle. It's what you ride on a ranch."

"Or four-wheelers. I understand a lot of ranchers use them in lieu of horses, nowadays." She snapped her fingers in a Lena show of temper. "Get with the times, cowboy."

He chuckled. "I assume that's the Lena we all know and love."

Angel smirked. "I was just getting into the part when you figured it out."

Duke started up a trail that led through a pass between two hills. The path grew narrower and the slopes steeper, falling off to the right.

Angel held onto the saddle horn. "I sure hope this horse knows what the hell he's doing."

"They're sure-footed. The thing to remember is to stay in the saddle."

She snorted. "Easy for you to say. I have a feeling this horse has a mind of his own. And he doesn't seem to like me on his back."

Hollywood blew out a whinny and shook his mane.

Angel nodded. "See?"

Duke glanced back over his shoulder, his brows furrowing. "If you're that uncomfortable riding, you can ride double with me."

"No, thank you. I like having my own saddle horn to hang onto and stirrups to stand in."

. . .

THEY RODE for the next hour without speaking.

Duke glanced back often, worried about Angel. Hell, he hadn't been riding for a long time, and his ass was getting sore in the saddle. He could imagine how tired Angel would be when they reached the cabin.

Around noon, he stopped at the creek Lyle had said he'd find. He dismounted and reached up to help Angel down from her horse.

She swung her leg over and dropped down into his arms.

For a moment he held her, letting her get her feet under her, and well, really just held her. The woman hadn't complained since they'd left the barn. She was tough and willing to do things the hard way. "How are you holding up?"

"I'll let you know when we get there." She glanced around. "Right now, I'm as hungry as a horse." She patted Hollywood's neck. "I think we're starting to bond."

Hollywood tossed his head and backed away a step.

"Fine, we're not bonding. At least he hasn't tried to dump me off the side of a cliff and run back to the barn. I call that progress."

Duke chuckled and slapped her bottom.

"Hey!" She rubbed her backside. "Why don't they make saddles cushioned?"

"They wouldn't last very long."

"Yeah, well they should."

With a smile on his face, Duke pulled out sandwiches he'd packed in the saddle bags and handed her one.

She ate standing, refusing to settle onto a nearby boulder.

"Have you seen any signs of a tail?" she asked.

Duke shook his head. "No signs yet. I'm hoping he won't be that close behind us. It will give us time to get to the cabin first and set up some early warning devices.

She nodded, chewing as she looked around. "This would be nice if we weren't on a mission."

"Perhaps when this is all said and done, we'll be allowed to come back for a real vacation." As soon as the words were out of his mouth, Duke realized what his words implied. He wanted and expected to continue to see Angel after his two weeks of bodyguard duty ended. But that might not be the case.

"Are you headed back to Hollywood at the end of the two weeks?" he asked.

Angel finished off the last bite of her sandwich and wiped the crumbs off her hands onto her jeans. "I don't know. I'm not sure how many more stunts my body can withstand." She smiled at him over her shoulder. "I'm not getting any younger."

Duke stepped behind her and circled her waist with his arms, pulling her back against his front.

"You make yourself sound old. What are you, twenty-seven?"

"See how much you know. I'm twenty-nine. I'll be thirty in three months."

"Ever think of staying in Montana?"

She leaned her head on his shoulder. "Hadn't crossed my mind. But I can see why people like it here. It's beautiful."

"Yes, it is." He kissed her temple. "Beautiful—"

The sound of a branch snapping made Duke freeze.

Hollywood whickered and tossed his head.

Duke's horse answered and pulled against his reins tied to a tree limb.

Duke shoved Angel behind him and drew his pistol from the holster on his hip.

Angel drew her weapon, too, and backed toward a tree. She held on to Duke's shirt, leading him back with her until they were both near enough to duck for cover.

"Are we being paranoid?" She stood beside him, facing the opposite direction.

"Hell, no." Now that they were out in the woods, just the two of them and one sick bastard preying on them, Duke was rethinking his assertion that he and Angel could handle this guy on their own.

At least not yet. They weren't in a defensive position, nor could they see the enemy coming.

Until they had a clear field of vision and fire, they were still on the prey side of the equation.

Silence reined, and the horses settled. Nothing moved but the swish of the horses' tails.

"Ready to move on?"

Angel nodded. "Ready."

"Think you can mount on your own?"

She bit her bottom lip, and then squared her shoulders. "Yes. Remember Hollywood and I have an understanding."

"Then let's get moving. I want to get set up long before dusk."

"Agreed."

"I'll be right back."

Angel waited while Duke strode quickly across the clearing to the where the horses were secured. He untied both sets of reins and walked the horses back to the trees. He looped the reins over Hollywood's neck and held the bridle while Angel mounted. Once she landed in the saddle, he swung up on his horse. "Lean over the horse's neck. You'll make less of a target."

She nodded.

He nudged his horse into a gallop and raced to the path.

Hollywood followed, easily keeping pace.

Angel held onto the saddle horn, leaning close to the horse's neck.

Once they rounded a bend in the trail, Duke

slowed his horse to manage the winding trail to the cabin.

Within another hour, they arrived at the cabin, quickly dismounted and unloaded the duffel bag from the back of Duke's horse.

Angel managed to dismount on her own and led the horse to a small corral several feet away from the cabin.

Once inside, Duke pulled all of the cans off the shelf and handed them and a can opener to Angel. "Open them halfway and empty the contents."

While she did that, he hurried to a nearby creek, with one of the cooking pots and scooped up pebbles from the creek bed.

When he got back to the cabin, Angel had all of the cans empty and had started poking holes in the sides with a pocket knife.

His heart swelled. He hadn't had to tell Angel what he was doing with the cans. She'd instinctively known.

Duke strung them together with long lengths of fishing line. Angel poured a few pebbles into each can and bent their lids closed.

When they were done, they carried their makeshift, early warning system out twenty yards deep into the woods around the periphery of the camp. Crouching in the brush, they watched and listened for several minutes for sounds of movement.

When Duke was as certain as he could be that they were alone, he strung the cans between the trees, setting the fishing line just high enough off the ground it would catch a foot passing through.

Once they'd strung the lines all around the perimeter, Duke and Angel returned to the cabin.

"You know we can't stay here, right?" Duke handed her a radio headset and settled one on his head.

She slipped the radio on and tapped the mic. "I know."

He could hear her voice through the radio in his ear and it made him feel a little better about positioning themselves on either side of the clearing.

He whispered into the mic, "There are bears and wolves in these woods."

Angel nodded, acknowledging that she could hear him through the radio, and then patted her handgun and lifted one of the M4A1 rifles. "We'll be ready. The early warning system will inform us about two and four-legged creatures."

He held up a hand for a high-five. "Let's do this." When she slapped his hand, he grabbed hers and pulled her close. "Don't be a hero, and keep your head down. It's not often I find a woman who speaks my language and looks as good as you do in body armor."

"You're not so bad yourself. I don't suppose

you'd consider going out on a date with me when this is all over?"

Duke closed his eyes and heaved a sigh. "There you go, being all macho. I'm supposed to ask *you* out."

"We're in a bit of a hurry, and you took too long." She held his hand up to her cheek. "It was a yes or no question."

"Yes."

Her face blossomed in a smile. "Good. Now that we have that settled, let's catch us a bad guy."

Duke shook his head. "I'm glad I never had a problem taking orders from a woman. In fact, I kind of like it when you order me around." He pulled her into his arms, guns and all and kissed her.

She returned the kiss with equal force and passion.

When they broke apart, she stared at him, her smile gone. "Do me a favor and don't die on me, will you?"

His heart pinched hard in his chest at the look in her eyes. "I'm going to be around for a long time. I have a date with a pretty girl. I refuse to disappoint her."

CHAPTER 9

DUKE LEFT the cabin through the front door. Angel waited a minute or two and sneaked out the back door, and then ducked into the brush. Once in the shadows, she stuck leaves and strands of grass into the back of her shirt and in her hair and smeared dirt on her face.

When she was sufficiently camouflaged, she worked her way around to the position she and Duke had agreed would be hers. There, she burrowed into the leaves and brush, careful not to point her weapons in Duke's direction. "In position."

"In position," he responded.

Angel lay with her rifle ready, her pistol within easy reach and waited.

Minutes passed into an hour. She shifted slightly several times, to keep her arms and legs from falling to sleep. Just when Angel began to think the joke was on them and their stalker wasn't that interested in following them into the mountains, Duke spoke in her ear.

"I'm going to the cabin to light a lantern."

"I've got your back," Angel said.

Duke slipped around the edge of the perimeter to the trail leading in from the creek. He emerged as if he'd been at the creek all along and was on his way back to spend the night in the cabin.

Angel held her breath until he entered the cabin. She released her breath, thankful he'd made it into the cabin and no shots had been fired.

A minute went by, then another.

Alternating her attention on the cabin and in the direction of the path leading up the hill to the clearing where the cabin stood, she almost didn't see the arrow until it arched toward the cabin roof.

For an instant, she wondered what the hell an arrow was going to do against a solid wood cabin. Then it hit the roof and an explosion blew out the windows and knocked the door off its hinges. Smoke and flames rose from the structure, billowing into the air.

Angel gasped and started to rise.

The rattle of pebbles in cans alerted her to movement near her.

She swung her rifle in the direction of the noise in time to see what appeared to be a shaggy bush hunkered low, moving through the brush fast, heading toward her position and zigzagging back and forth.

With her heart lodged in her throat, not knowing whether Duke had made it out of the cabin before the explosion, Angel zeroed in on the bastard and pulled the trigger.

As the bullet left the barrel, the attacker dodged right, raised a camouflaged rifle and aimed at her.

Angel fired again, hitting him in the arm as he fired a round.

A bullet whizzed past her ear and hit the tree behind her, sending chunks of bark showering down on her.

The man hit the ground with a grunt, rolled over with his weapon and aimed directly at Angel.

She flung herself to the left at the same time as a shot rang out. Landing hard on the butt of her rifle, she gasped as pain shot through her rib. For a moment, she thought she'd been hit, but she didn't care. The bastard had to die, or he'd kill her.

She rolled over several times to get away from her previous position and behind a log lying on the ground. When she stopped, she glanced over the top of the log.

Her attacker had assumed a kneeling position, his weapon aiming toward the log behind which she hid.

"You're nothing but a cold-hearted bitch, Lena Love."

"Is that right, Myles?" Angel called out, betting on the attacker being Lena's ex-boyfriend. "You think you're some big bad hunter, but all you've ever done is kill caged animals."

"You hired a bodyguard to protect you, but I killed him, too."

Angel's stomach knotted. She refused to believe Duke was dead. He'd promised to go out on a date with her. A Delta Force soldier's promise was sacred. He'd keep it, damn it. She blinked her stinging eyes. For a moment, silence filled the air. In the distance, the hum of an aircraft engine echoed through the mountains, and smoke drifted through the air.

Duke had yet to turn up, leading Angel to believe he could be dead or dying in the burning cabin. She had to do something to force Myles's hand and get this over with so that she could find Duke.

"Hey Myles, were you afraid my bodyguard was better in bed than you? Is that why you felt a need to kill him?" she taunted. "Because he *was. So* much better...and *bigger.*" In Angel's mind, a man who had to kill defenseless, endangered animals purely for sport, had to have a little dick.

"Bitch." Myles fired at the log, knocking a notch

in the top, far too close to Angel's head for her comfort.

"That's my date you're calling names," a voice shouted in the distance and into Angel's headset.

Her heart leaped with joy.

Duke!

She heard the shot and looked up in time to see Myles fall to the ground. He rolled over to his side and reached for his rifle lying in the dirt not far from where he'd landed.

Another shot rang out hitting Myles again, this time in the gut. Lena's ex-boyfriend lay groaning in the dirt.

Angel left the cover of her log, ran toward Myles and grabbed his rifle, flinging it away.

Not that he would need it anymore, he wasn't going far with three bullets in him.

Duke appeared beside her. "Did you shoot that last shot?"

"No. I thought you did." She flung her arms around him. "I thought you were dead."

He chuckled and hugged her to him. "Deltas don't die that easily."

She leaned back and stared up at him. "How did you get out of the house?"

He grinned. "Same way you did—through the back door. And none too soon."

She rose on her toes and kissed him. "You

scared the crap out of me. I didn't know whether or not you were in that cabin when it blew."

A shadow fell over Angel and Duke.

They glanced up at the same time to see a man dangling from a parachute, a rifle in his hand. As he neared the trees, he adjusted the pitch of the chute, angling toward the clearing near the smoldering cabin. He landed on his feet, gathered his chute and moved out of the way as another man and parachute spiraled downward toward the clearing, and still another.

Duke grabbed Angel's arm and hurried her toward what ended up being four men, folding their chutes, all carrying military-grade rifles.

Angel dug her heels in the dirt, refusing to step out into the clearing "Are you sure they're friendly?"

"Friendly?" Duke laughed out loud. "These men are my brothers."

Her frown eased only slightly. "Brothers? I assumed you were an only child."

He dragged her toward the one who'd landed first, and whose bullet had been the one to end Myles's hunting expeditions permanently.

"Rider!" Duke dropped her arm and engulfed the man and his parachute harness in a bear hug.

The man he'd called Rider pounded him on his back. "And to think, we almost missed the party." He glanced over Duke's shoulder at Angel. "Aren't you going to introduce me to your client?" His gaze went to the rifle she carried and the sticks and twigs she'd stuck in her hair. "Since when did movie stars start carrying rifles and shooting bad guys other than on sets with blank rounds?"

"Rider, this isn't Lena Love, though she's the spitting image of the movie star. This is her stunt double and former Army Ranger, Angel Carson."

"Should have known Duke was having way too much fun without us. We got here just in time." Rider held out his hand to Angel.

"Nice to meet you." When she placed her hand in his, he didn't shake it. Instead, he pulled her into his arms and hugged her.

Duke grabbed Rider's shoulder and pulled him away from Angel. "Hey, get your grubby hands off my girl. You have Briana, now."

"And I don't want any other woman. But I'm happy you found a woman who can hold her own in a gunfight." Rider grinned at Angel. "I can't wait to introduce you to Briana. She's going to love you."

Another man joined them. "Duke, what's this? You've only been here a couple of days, and you've already found a woman?" He turned to Angel and held out his hand. "By the way, I'm Blaze, this dirt bag's teammate. I guess Duke's joined a different kind of team altogether." He winked. "A better looking team."

Duke's cheeks reddened.

Angel loved that Duke was embarrassed and couldn't help giving him even more hell than his buddies were. "Hey, don't I have a say in whose woman I am?"

All five men turned toward her.

"You mean you're not Duke's?" Rider asked. He looked past her to the man lying on the ground, moaning. "Tell me that's not your guy.

Angel and Duke replied as one. "No!"

Duke slipped an arm around Angel. "Give us a chance. I owe this woman a night out. Now that we've taken care of Lena's ex-boyfriend, we might just get to go on that date. Then she can decide whether or not she wants a man, and if that man could possibly be me."

"Well, don't let us get in the way of true love. We've each got a date with a fishing pole. Point us to the nearest stream, and we'll get out of the way."

"Be happy to," Duke said. "After we put out the fire and get Lena's ex off the mountain."

"Oh, so now we have to work for the right to fish?" Blaze shook his head. "Fine. Let's do this and get to our mini vacation before we have to head back."

Duke's friends helped load Myles onto Hollywood's saddle. Then they loaded their parachutes onto the other saddle and headed down the mountain, leading the horses.

Duke walked beside Angel, trailing behind the others. "The guys are just kidding about you being my woman."

"Oh, that's too bad." She leaned into him. "I was kind of liking the idea."

"Yeah?" Duke's face brightened. "It's never wise for a man to assume anything, especially about a woman who can fire a rifle almost as well as he can."

She jabbed him in the gut. "*Better* than he can."

"You nicked the guy in the leg," he reminded her.

Her lips quirked on the corners. "I was *aiming* for the leg."

"You win." He pulled her into his embrace and lifted her chin. "But in the end...I win."

"How so?"

"I got the girl."

"You did?" she said, her voice barely a whisper, her gaze sinking to his mouth.

"Yup." Then he kissed her, claiming her, making her his with that single caress.

When she pulled away, she said, "You'll get no argument from me, as long as you keep kissing me like that."

"Deal." And he kissed her again. Under the big sky of Montana, on a trail in the Crazy Mountains, in front of his band of brothers, Duke had staked his claim on Angel.

She couldn't have been happier. And he owed her a date. She would insist on the location. A place that had a king-sized bed with a cotton-candy-pink comforter and a drawer full of protection.

They still had the majority of the two weeks to enjoy Lena's hospitality. She planned on making the most of it…with Duke.

MONTANA RANGER

BROTHERHOOD PROTECTORS BOOK #5

New York Times & *USA Today*
Bestselling Author

ELLE JAMES

New York Times & USA Today Bestselling Author
ELLE JAMES
MONTANA
RANGER
BROTHERHOOD PROTECTORS

CHAPTER 1

"ARE you sure you don't want me to stay?" Gavin Blackstock straightened, after hooking up the mower to the oldest tractor on the Brighter Days Rehabilitation Ranch. He shook his shaggy black hair out of his gray eyes and wiped the grease from his hands.

Hannah Kendricks sighed. Yeah, she wished Gavin could stay and cut the hayfield instead of her, but...

"No, we need the supplies and tomorrow is Sunday. The feed stores are closed." She stared at the aging farm machinery, wondering if it would conk out in the middle of the field and leave her to walk all the way back to the barn. "I'll keep the tractor going long enough to cut the hay." She held up her hand as if being sworn into office. "Don't worry, I promise to baby it."

"Why don't you let Percy do the cutting?" Gavin suggested.

"I would, but he's better at manning the baler. The hay I cut three days ago is dry and ready to bale. If we want to get all of it baled by Wednesday, we need to cut today."

Gavin opened his mouth to protest.

Hannah held up her hand. "We've got it covered. I hired three hands to help."

"Troy Nash got here early this morning." Gavin frowned. "Why did you hire that boy?"

"I heard he'd been fired from his job at the feed store. I figured he could use the money since his daddy had his heart attack."

"You've got a soft spot for those down and out."

She shrugged. "We take care of our neighbors in these parts."

"Yeah, but Troy's a known troublemaker."

"Maybe he just needs someone to believe in him." Hannah ran her hand across the smooth seat of one of the saddles stacked on a saddletree. "Besides, I hired Abe and Mark. They're good, hard-working teenagers. Don't worry about us."

"Why the hurry? If it doesn't get cut today, we can do it tomorrow when I'm here to help."

Glancing up at the bright Montana sky, Hannah shook her head. "A storm's headed our way from off the Washington coast. You know as well as I do that we can't bale it if it's wet. And if we don't cut the field now, the hay won't have time to dry and be baled before the storm hits."

"So?"

Hannah's lips tightened. "You know we need two cuttings from those fields to keep us from having to buy hay to get us through the winter."

Gavin glanced at the old tractor. "This hunk of junk gets crankier every time we use it. I brought it up to Holloway when he was here last month, but I'll mention it again. He's supposed to be here tomorrow."

Hannah bit down on her bottom lip. Holloway was the young financial manager of the Brighter Days Rehabilitation Ranch. He showed up once a month to do the accounting and make any big buying decisions. Otherwise, he left the ranch for Hannah to run as she saw fit, making the day-to-day hiring, firing and maintenance decisions. "He can be pretty tight with the purse strings."

"Maybe you can turn on some of the charm you reserve for our clients." Gavin cocked his brows.

Hannah glanced down at her faded shirt and jeans and gave her best friend a very unladylike snort. "I'm not very convincing as a girl."

Gavin laughed out loud. "Don't knock yourself, Hannah. From where I stand, you're all female. And you do it better than most women I know."

"Yeah, but where Holloway comes from, I'm nowhere near the kind of woman he's used to dealing with. I don't even know how to bat my lashes." To prove it, she fluttered her eyelashes. The action felt as clumsy as it probably looked based on Gavin's grimace.

"Yeah, don't do that. It just looks weird." He limped to the truck. "Just try to be nice."

Hannah followed. "I'll see what I can do. We really need at least one newer tractor before next season." She hugged Gavin. "Thanks for giving it your best shot. At least, it's running."

"Hopefully, it will remain running until you get through the cutting." Gavin glanced toward the barn. "Looks like Percy has his team of helpers ready. I'd better get to Eagle Rock and back so that I can be of some assistance before the day's over." He gave Hannah a stern glance. "Be careful out there. We don't want any more 'accidents'. We can't lose our best therapist."

"Your *only* therapist," Hannah muttered. "I'll be all right. Quit worrying. What happened recently was just a couple of accidents. They could have happened to anyone." She gripped Gavin's arm and stared directly into his eyes. "There's no conspiracy going on here at Brighter Days."

Frowning, he touched her cheek. "I'm not so sure. You're the only one the accidents have affected." He drew in a deep breath, released it and nodded. "I should stay and do the cutting."

"Go." Hannah gave Gavin a gentle shove. "I can

handle this. And nobody is going to mess with me. I want to be here for the guys. Once I finish the field, I'll help load hay on the truck and trailer. I need to be there to watch and make sure none of them does anything that will set them back on their roads to recovery."

"Yes, you do need to be there. They wouldn't be nearly as far along as they are without your help." He glanced down at his leg. "I never thought I'd walk again, and look where I am, because of you."

Hannah's chest expanded. Nothing was more rewarding than helping wounded veterans regain mobility and some semblance of a life worth living.

Working at the Brighter Days Rehab Ranch, she got the best of both worlds. She got to help people, like her best friend from childhood, and give former soldiers, sailors, Marines and airmen a reason to keep fighting, for a great cause—rehabilitating horses rescued from horrible situations.

And she wouldn't have had this opportunity if not for the benevolence of the investment group that had purchased the ranch and allowed her to make it into the thriving therapy center it was.

Gavin paused before climbing into the truck. "Oh, and Hannah, you might want to think about being the girl you are and date or find someone to love. You need a life outside of this ranch."

"Says the man who hasn't had a date in over a year?" She shook her head. "I'll date when you date." Narrowing her eyes, Hannah tilted her head. "Maybe I'll date you."

Gavin gave her a twisted smile. "Thanks, but it would be like dating my little sister. No can do."

Hannah nodded. They'd tried kissing, once, but the sparks weren't there and the connection didn't feel right. Like Gavin said, it was like kissing a sibling. Bleh! "You're right. We weren't made for each other in that way. Why spoil a perfect friendship? But that doesn't mean you can't find a woman to love you and all of your faults."

Gavin crossed his arms over his chest. "Same to you, Han. Same to you. I'll date if you date."

"Watch what you dare. I've been known to rise to a challenge."

"I'm counting on it." He stood for a moment longer and then dropped his arms. "Go cut the hay, but don't forget…I dared you."

As Gavin climbed into the farm truck and spun around on the gravel, heading for town, Hannah watched, something tugged at her heart, telling her that Gavin had a point. Since she'd left college, she hadn't been on a date. Perhaps it was time.

Ranch foreman, Percy Pearson, appeared from around the side of the barn on the ranch's other tractor, towing the hay baler. He waved as he passed Hannah. "Ready?"

She nodded, climbed onto the old tractor's seat and waited for the farm truck, driven by medically retired Staff Sergeant Lori Mize, to pass. A motley crew of wounded warriors and hired hands filled the bed of the pickup, laughing and joking about the work ahead. She hoped between the group of able-bodied hired hands—Troy, Abe and Mark—and the three veterans—Franklin, Vasquez and Young, with their varying degrees of disabilities—they'd get the work done quickly.

Hannah started the engine and shifted the tractor into first gear. Resigning herself to a long day in the field, she adjusted her cowboy hat over her forehead and drove the tractor through the gate into the pasture. The clear sky promised to turn the cool Montana morning into a warm, early summer day. Hopefully, free of strange accidents.

Cookie, the ranch cook, waved and closed the gate behind her. He always stuck around for the warriors who weren't ready, or weren't capable of the heavy lifting needed to throw fifty- to eighty-pound hay bales onto the trailer. Not that they had any other veterans staying behind. All men and women were on deck that day. Cookie would have a huge meal waiting when they returned, tired and starving, having burned a ton of calories.

Hannah followed Percy until she came to the field she was to cut that day.

He pressed on to the one farther out, taking with him the truck with the crew that would load what he baled.

Hannah would spend the day alone, driving the tractor with the mower on the back. This particular field had its share of hills. She hoped and prayed the old tractor wouldn't bog down and give up while climbing the hills, and that the brakes would hold on the way down.

Starting at the far end with the steepest slopes, Hannah worked her way up and down the hill. She kept a steady pace, careful not to push the tractor's engine too hard. On the way down the hill, she moved as slowly as she could, shifting into low gear to let the engine help, rather than relying totally on the worn brakes.

After the first pass, she felt more confident the tractor would handle the job. She settled back in her seat and let her mind wander away from the hayfield.

Hannah thought about how far she'd come and how satisfied she was with where she'd landed in her life. Growing up on this ranch as the daughter of the owner's housekeeper, she'd learned to ride a horse almost before she'd learned to walk.

She'd never known her father. Her mother had instilled in her a love for the outdoors and ranch life. And she had all the male role models she needed to teach her what was expected of a man and how he should behave toward a woman. Preferring the outdoors to housework, Hannah had grown up working alongside the cowboys and ranch hands, doing everything they did to care for the animals, buildings and land.

Her mother had insisted she go to college, scrounging and saving so that her daughter wouldn't have to take out loans to pay for her tuition.

Hannah would rather have stayed at the ranch and worked with the horses, but she knew a college education meant a lot to her mother, so she'd gone.

Gavin, her best friend from high school, had joined the Marines and gone to fight in the Middle East. Two years into his enlistment, Gavin had been injured in battle, taking a hit to his leg. He'd come back to the States where he'd undergone multiple surgeries in an attempt to remove all the shrapnel, repair the damage and save the leg. Finally, they'd had to amputate below his knee. Once he'd lost his leg, he'd been fitted with a prosthetic and sent to rehabilitation therapy to learn how to deal with his loss. After several months, Gavin was medically retired and sent home where he struggled with depression and trying to fit into a place where he felt he no longer belonged.

Hannah had been on the fence about what to study. When she'd gone to visit her best friend in the hospital, and later in physical therapy, she'd made her decision. She wanted to help people like Gavin regain use of their limbs, or learn how to get along without them, and in the process, regain their independence, confidence and self-respect.

She'd studied hard so that she would be accepted into the physical therapy program and graduated at the top of her class. Her mother had been so proud.

She'd taken a position at a rehab center in Bozeman, working with people who'd had knee and hip replacements, rotator cuff surgeries and more. But she wanted to work with veterans.

Gavin had stayed in DC, looking for a job. He couldn't find anything that suited him. He liked being around horses more than people, but he still felt drawn to his comrades in the Marines, wishing he could be back in battle, helping to fight for his country.

Hannah had applied to work at Walter Reed in Bethesda, Maryland. The same day she'd received an invitation to interview, her mother had suffered a fatal stroke.

Though three years had passed, the pain of her loss still pinched Hannah's chest.

She pulled her mind out of her memories as she reached the end of the row. Turning the tractor, she started mowing the next row, heading down a hill toward a ravine lined with trees. The rhythmic chug of the engine lured her back into her memories.

Her mother died the day after her stroke, never

having regained consciousness. Hannah had delayed her interview in Bethesda for two weeks to give herself time to arrange for her mother's funeral and to settle her affairs. She'd buried her mother, her only living relative, in the cemetery outside Eagle Rock, the nearest town to the ranch her mother had called home.

Percy and Gavin had stood by her side, along with the handful of ranch workers and the ranch owner, Mr. Lansing. They'd buried her mother on an ironically bright, sunny Montana day. She would have loved the sunshine.

In a domino effect, Mr. Lansing had a heart attack that night and ended up in a long-term care facility. Percy and Hannah knew the event was the beginning of the end of their little hodge-podge family of ranch workers.

Her heart heavy, Hannah had said her goodbyes to Gavin and the ranch hands. Then she'd entered the ranch house, packed up what she would keep of her mother's and arranged for the rest to be donated. Heartsick and so sad she could barely breathe, she'd set her suitcases by the front door, with the intention of leaving the ranch in the morning.

That's when Percy had come to her. Someone had asked to speak with her on the telephone.

She hadn't wanted to, but Percy insisted it was

important—something to do with the sale of the ranch.

With a knife twisting in her heart, she'd taken the call. An attorney requested a meeting with her the following day. He had information about her mother's will and news about the sale of the ranch.

Reluctantly, she'd agreed to meet him at his office in Eagle Rock the next morning before she left town.

Hannah's lips lifted. Even from the grave, her mother had been looking out for her. She must have known the day would come soon when Mr. Lansing couldn't manage the ranch. He didn't have any heirs, and he'd need to sell. She'd left Hannah her life savings, a modest amount of money stashed away in the bank for her own retirement she'd never see. And she'd left a letter for Hannah.

Dear Hannah,

If you're reading this letter, I've managed to die before I had a chance to tell you about your father. I didn't talk to you about him as you grew up, but I wanted you to know he was a good man. I never told him about you, so don't blame him for not being a part of your life. Blame me. Maybe I didn't make the right decision by not telling you about him, but I felt it was the right one for you and for him. Just don't hate your father. And no matter what, I have always and will always love you with all of my heart. Love, Mom

Hannah barely heard the rest of what the lawyer had to say, so deep was she in her own misery.

He paused, expecting an answer to a question she hadn't absorbed.

Clutching the letter to her chest, she looked up and asked him to repeat it.

"Will you stay and help manage the transition from cattle ranch to a rehabilitation ranch for wounded warriors and sick or injured horses?"

Hannah blinked. "Who? Me?"

The lawyer nodded, repeating the proposition presented by the new owners of the ranch. "He—they want you to think about it." The lawyer leaned forward and touched her arm, his brows furrowed with obvious concern. "If you stay, the other employees will keep their jobs and you could do a whole lot of good for veterans and animals."

Stunned, she left his office in a daze and returned to the ranch where Percy met her with his duffel bag in hand.

He set down the bag and gripped her arms. "Hannah, are you okay?"

She nodded and then said, "Percy, I've been so wrapped up in my own grief, I didn't stop to think about you. What are you going to do when this ranch sells?"

He shrugged. "I don't know. I thought I'd head out to my sister's place in North Dakota."

"But you hate going to your sister's for more than a day…two tops."

"It's the only place I know to go." He forced a smile. "But don't worry about me. I always land on my feet."

She tilted her head and given him a stern stare. "You've worked here as long as I can remember. When was the last time you had to look for a job?"

He glanced away. "It's been about thirty years or so."

For the first time, Hannah noticed the gray in his brown hair and the deeply grooved lines around his eyes. The man had leathery skin from years in the sun and weather and he had to be closing in on sixty years old. Who would hire him?

Staring at her old friend, the man who'd been the closest thing to a father she'd had, Hannah had made her decision. "We're staying."

Her lips curled at the memory of Percy's expression when he realized he wouldn't have to go to his sister in North Dakota. She'd called Gavin the next day and begged him to come work for the Brighter Days Rehabilitation Ranch where he could help veterans and horses. He'd be doing his part for his brothers and sisters-in-arms.

Hannah pressed her foot on the tractor's brakes as the hill dipped sharply toward the ravine. She'd made the turn on the previous pass with no problem.

But something snapped, making a clanking sound of metal hitting metal, and the brakes failed.

Hannah's heart jumped to her throat. Instead of slowing, the tractor picked up speed, the weight of the tractor plus the mower, pushing it even faster down the hill.

Hannah's fingers tightened on the steering wheel and her pulse raced. She debated turning to slow the vehicle in its headlong rush toward the ravine. But turning at that pace was a surefire way to flip the tractor.

She tried to shift to a lower speed to let the tractor engine slow her descent, but no matter how hard she shoved the lever, it wouldn't shift to low. Her gut clenched as she ran out of options.

With trees and rocks waiting for her to crash into them, Hannah had no other choice but to get off. Her only problem was, if she jumped, she stood a strong chance of landing in the mower. At which point she'd be cut to pieces.

She stared at the trees and rocks ahead, her mind working through the scenarios at lightning speed, survival instincts kicking in.

That's when she spotted her only chance. The option was risky, but slightly less risky than crashing into the ravine. She turned the tractor's steering wheel ever so slightly, careful not to cause it to flip, and angled it toward a large tree with a long branch hanging just low enough for her to reach out and snag it with her arms.

Hannah held on to the steering wheel, fighting to keep it headed toward the tree, wondering if she could pull off what she planned.

With no time left to change her mind, she released the steering wheel, pushed to her feet and threw both arms over the branch.

Her chest crashed into the solid limb, knocking the air from her lungs. But she held on.

The tractor and mower continued on their course straight toward a large boulder, smashing into it with enough force that the front end of the tractor crumpled. Momentum carried the mower forward, flipping it up and over the top of the trac-tor, crushing the seat where Hannah had sat moments before.

All of these actions happened in a matter of seconds. Hannah's arms slipped on the rough tree bark and she fell from her perch, landing on her back. Pain shot through her head and darkness enveloped her.

ABOUT THE AUTHOR

ELLE JAMES also writing as MYLA JACKSON is a *New York Times* and *USA Today* Bestselling author of books including cowboys, intrigues and paranormal adventures that keep her readers on the edges of their seats. When she's not at her computer, she's traveling, snow skiing, boating, or riding her ATV, dreaming up new stories. Learn more about Elle James at www.ellejames.com

Website | Facebook | Twitter | GoodReads | Newsletter | BookBub | Amazon

Or visit her alter ego Myla Jackson at mylajackson.com
Website | Facebook | Twitter | Newsletter

Follow Me!
www.ellejames.com
ellejames@ellejames.com

ALSO BY ELLE JAMES

Iron Horse Legacy

Soldier's Duty (#1)

Ranger's Baby (#2)

Marine's Promise (#3)

SEAL's Vow (#4)

Warrior's Resolve (#5)

Brotherhood Protectors Series

Montana SEAL (#1)

Bride Protector SEAL (#2)

Montana D-Force (#3)

Cowboy D-Force (#4)

Montana Ranger (#5)

Montana Dog Soldier (#6)

Montana SEAL Daddy (#7)

Montana Ranger's Wedding Vow (#8)

Montana SEAL Undercover Daddy (#9)

Cape Cod SEAL Rescue (#10)

Montana SEAL Friendly Fire (#11)

Montana SEAL's Mail-Order Bride (#12)

SEAL Justice (#13)

Mission: Six

One Intrepid SEAL

Two Dauntless Hearts

Three Courageous Words

Four Relentless Days

Five Ways to Surrender

Six Minutes to Midnight

Hearts & Heroes Series

Wyatt's War (#1)

Mack's Witness (#2)

Ronin's Return (#3)

Sam's Surrender (#4)

Take No Prisoners Series

SEAL's Honor (#1)

SEAL'S Desire (#2)

SEAL's Embrace (#3)

SEAL's Obsession (#4)

SEAL's Proposal (#5)

SEAL's Seduction (#6)

SEAL'S Defiance (#7)

SEAL's Deception (#8)

SEAL's Deliverance (#9)

SEAL's Ultimate Challenge (#10)

Texas Billionaire Club

Tarzan & Janine (#1)

Something To Talk About (#2)

Who's Your Daddy (#3)

Love & War (#4)

Ballistic Cowboy

Hot Combat (#1)

Hot Target (#2)

Hot Zone (#3)

Hot Velocity (#4)

Cajun Magic Mystery Series

Voodoo on the Bayou (#1)

Voodoo for Two (#2)

Deja Voodoo (#3)

Cajun Magic Mysteries Books 1-3

Billionaire Online Dating Service

The Billionaire Husband Test (#1)

The Billionaire Cinderella Test (#2)

The Billionaire Bride Test (#3)

The Billionaire Daddy Test (#4)

The Billionaire Matchmaker Test (#5)

SEAL Of My Own

Navy SEAL Survival

Navy SEAL Captive

Navy SEAL To Die For

Navy SEAL Six Pack

Devil's Shroud Series

Deadly Reckoning (#1)

Deadly Engagement (#2)

Deadly Liaisons (#3)

Deadly Allure (#4)

Deadly Obsession (#5)

Deadly Fall (#6)

Covert Cowboys Inc Series

Triggered (#1)

Taking Aim (#2)

Bodyguard Under Fire (#3)

Cowboy Resurrected (#4)

Navy SEAL Justice (#5)

Navy SEAL Newlywed (#6)

High Country Hideout (#7)

Clandestine Christmas (#8)

Thunder Horse Series

Hostage to Thunder Horse (#1)

Thunder Horse Heritage (#2)

Thunder Horse Redemption (#3)

Christmas at Thunder Horse Ranch (#4)

Demon Series

Hot Demon Nights (#1)

Demon's Embrace (#2)

Tempting the Demon (#3)

Lords of the Underworld

Witch's Initiation (#1)

Witch's Seduction (#2)

The Witch's Desire (#3)

Possessing the Witch (#4)

Stealth Operations Specialists (SOS)

Nick of Time

Alaskan Fantasy

Blown Away

Stranded

Feel the Heat

The Heart of a Cowboy

Protecting His Heroine

Warrior's Conquest

Rogues

Enslaved by the Viking Short Story

Conquests

Smokin' Hot Firemen

Love on the Rocks

Protecting the Colton Bride

Protecting the Colton Bride & Colton's Cowboy Code

Heir to Murder

Secret Service Rescue

High Octane Heroes

Haunted

Engaged with the Boss

Cowboy Brigade

Time Raiders: The Whisper

Bundle of Trouble

Killer Body

Operation XOXO

An Unexpected Clue

Baby Bling

Under Suspicion, With Child

Texas-Size Secrets

Cowboy Sanctuary

Lakota Baby

Dakota Meltdown

Beneath the Texas Moon

Made in the USA
Columbia, SC
16 April 2022

59082450R00096